RESCUE!

I plunged into the water. I didn't even take a breath.

I came up sputtering, choking.

Three long strokes, that's all it took to get to the girl.

Still coughing, I grabbed her blond hair, tugged it. Tugged her up. Pulled her face out of the water.

So heavy. Her head was so heavy.

I stared at it—stared at her face.

Stared at it and stared at it.

And didn't believe it.

Books by R. L. Stine

Available from ARCHWAY Paperbacks

FEAR STREET®
SUPER CHILLER
R·L·STINE

The Dead Lifeguard

A Parachute Press Book

AN ARCHWAY PAPERBACK
Published by POCKET BOOKS
New York   London   Toronto   Sydney   Tokyo   Singapore

This book is a work of fiction. Names, characters, places and incidents are either products of the author's imagination or are used fictitiously. Any resemblance to actual events or locales or persons, living or dead, is entirely coincidental.

AN ARCHWAY PAPERBACK *Original*

An Archway Paperback published by
POCKET BOOKS, a division of Simon & Schuster Inc.
1230 Avenue of the Americas, New York, NY 10020

Copyright © 1994 by Parachute Press, Inc.

ISBN: 0-671-86834-9

First Archway Paperback printing June 1994

10 9 8 7 6 5 4 3 2 1

FEAR STREET is a registered trademark of Parachute Press, Inc.

AN ARCHWAY PAPERBACK and colophon are registered trademarks of Simon & Schuster Inc.

Cover art by Bill Schmidt

Printed in the U.S.A.

IL 7+

PART ONE

A NEW GHOST

Chapter 1

MOUSE

*H*i, Terry. It's me. Mouse.

Yeah. It's me. Mouse. Are you surprised?

Can you hear me okay? There's a little static on the line.

What's up, Terry? How's it going?

I know you can't talk. So just listen—okay? You listening? Yeah. I know you are.

Hey, Terry, guess what? I passed the test.

What test, you ask.

The blood test! Ha-ha.

Just a joke, Terry. I passed the lifeguard test. Really! I'm going to be a lifeguard. Do you believe it, Mouse? A lifeguard!

It took a long time, huh? But I did it.

Well, come on, Terry. You knew I'd *kill* to become a lifeguard.

3

So I did it. Yeah. I killed a lifeguard. Ha-ha.

Why am I telling you?

Because I know you can't blow the whistle on me, Terry.

Ha-ha. Get it? Lifeguard? Blow the whistle? You always had a great sense of humor. Like me. I mean, that's why we were such good friends, right?

Hey, Terry, I know you can't talk. I mean, tell me something I don't know.

I know you're dead.

I know I'm talking to a dial tone here. I can hear the buzzing, you know.

I mean, I'm not crazy. You know me, right, Terry? You know I'm not crazy.

I know you're dead, Terry. And I know why you're dead.

Because of the lifeguards.

That's why I'm going to kill them. One by one.

For you, Terry. That's right. I'm going to do it for you. Because Mouse doesn't let a friend down.

Even if you're dead, Terry, you're still my friend. You'll always be my friend.

I just keep thinking about last summer. And the summer before that. I keep thinking and thinking. I can't stop. I can't stop even if I want to.

And that's how I know I have to kill the lifeguards.

Yeah. I know. I know you can't thank me.

Don't you think I hear the dial tone in my head? I've got good ears. I hear it.

I know you can't thank me. But don't worry about it.

I'll call you again. From the swim club. Up at North Beach.

Yeah, I know you're dead, Terry. You don't have to remind me. I'm not crazy, you know. No way.

Got to run. Later, okay?

Tell everyone Mouse says hi.

Yeah. Bye, Terry. Take care. Take care.

I'll do the rest.

Chapter 2

LINDSAY

I had packed in such a hurry, I forgot to bring any sunblock.

That was the thought that crossed my mind as I walked the four blocks from the bus stop to the front gate. It's funny how things pop into your mind. How you have no control over them.

What made me think of sunblock? Certainly not the sky. I gazed up at the heavy storm clouds, so low and dark. I heard the rumble of thunder in the distance. The gusting breeze was cool and wet.

I hope the storm passes quickly, I thought. Tomorrow is opening day. I want to sit at my lifeguard post and soak up the rays.

I dropped my heavy black duffel bag to the ground and stared up at the sign. NORTH BEACH COUNTRY CLUB.

Well, here we go, Lindsay, I told myself. Back again for another summer.

I rubbed my shoulder through my T-shirt. The duffel bag was heavy. I had stuffed practically everything I owned into it. Everything but sunblock.

What could I have been thinking of?

Escape, I guess. Escape for the whole summer. A summer to meet new people, make a fresh start. I mean, back in the lifeguard dorm, living with seven or eight other kids—it *had* to be outstanding!

Party time all summer long!

The front gate to the pool area was padlocked. I'd have to carry my stuff around to the side. Another low rumble of thunder—closer this time—made me realize I'd better hurry.

I gazed through the tall chain-link fence at the clubhouse. It appeared dull and black under the darkening sky.

The clubhouse was an endlessly long two-story redwood building. It was supposed to look like a forest lodge, I guess, only a hundred times bigger. The rows of windows stared back at me like blank, dark eyes.

Behind the clubhouse I glimpsed the swimming pool, the water flat and gray, reflecting the sky. Beyond that stretched the tennis courts.

I couldn't see the small guest house that was the lifeguard dorm. It was hidden by one wing of the clubhouse.

A jagged streak of lightning crackled overhead. A clap of thunder made me jump.

I hoisted my duffel bag to my shoulder and began to make my way to the side gate.

The black clouds all rolled together. Around them, the sky had become a sickly yellow. Strange light. The grass, the fence, the lodge—nothing was the right color.

Hurry, Lindsay, I urged myself. You don't want to look like a drenched alley cat when you meet the others.

My ragged white high-tops scraped along the pavement as I started to jog, bent under the weight of the duffel bag.

I suddenly wished I had a mirror. I had left home in such a mad rush, I hadn't had time to check my hair. Had I even brushed it?

As I walked, I fluffed it up with one hand. My hair is short and straight and blond. It almost always falls right into place. But I constantly worry about it anyway.

I know I'm usually pretty okay. I'm not beautiful or anything. My nose is too short and my face is too round. People always tell me I'm cute. I guess I don't mind.

I felt a cold sprinkle of rain on my forehead. Glancing up, I saw that the black clouds had completely covered the yellow sky now. A car rolled by, its headlights shining, even though it was still afternoon.

I shielded my eyes from the bright light until the car passed. Then I continued on to the side gate.

The tall chain-link fence shook in the wind. It made a vibrating sound, a steady hum.

Through the fence I saw the guest house, a small version of the main clubhouse. It was actually attached to one end of the clubhouse.

The swimming pool stretched near it. I could see splashes as raindrops hit the pool. There were lights on inside the guest house, and I could make out the back of a boy's head in one window.

Who is that? I wondered.

Who will the other lifeguards be this year? Will I know any of them? Will anyone be back from last summer?

The boy had red hair. His head bobbed up and down as he talked.

I felt another raindrop on my head. One on my shoulder, cold through my cotton T-shirt.

Shifting the duffel bag onto my other shoulder, I tried the gate.

Locked.

I shook it hard. It clattered noisily. A roar of thunder drowned out the clattering. The ground seemed to shake.

Rain pattered lightly on the pavement. The air had that tangy, sour smell that always comes just before a storm. The wind tore sharply, first from one direction, then back on itself.

I wished the redheaded boy would turn around and see me. Then maybe he'd run out to let me in.

I shook the gate again. Then I remembered my ID card.

The club had sent it to me when they okayed my application. It had my picture on it. Not a very good picture. Blurred, with me in my old haircut, my hair longer and sort of flipped over my shoulders.

They said all I had to do was run the card through

the slot by the gate, and the electronic lock would buzz open.

I set my duffel down, unzipped it, and searched for my wallet. I knew I had packed it on top.

The rain pattered steadily now. The raindrops were big. They hit the pavement with loud splashes. My hair was wet. My T-shirt was drenched.

I fumbled around till I found my red vinyl wallet, pulled it open, and took out the ID card.

A car rushed along the main road, catching me in its headlights for a minute. I searched for the metal box to run my card through. In the guest house window, the boy moved. Another boy appeared, his back also to the window.

Finally I found the box, about chest-high on the fence next to the gate. A tiny red light blinked on and off on the front. I slid my card slowly through the slot and waited to hear a buzzing sound.

Nothing.

The rain came down even harder, the fat drops splattering loudly.

I'm going to get soaked, I thought.

I shook my head hard, shaking water from my hair, and tried the card in the slot again.

Still nothing.

I turned the card over and ran it through the other way.

The red light blinked steadily. The gate didn't buzz open.

I let out a frustrated groan. What's wrong with the stupid gate? I asked myself.

The rain came down even harder. The wind blew it against the tall fence in sheets.

I was totally drenched. I rattled the gate.

I could see the two boys in the window of the guest house.

"Hey—can anyone hear me?" I shouted. "Hey!"

My voice was blown back by the wind, muffled behind the splatter of rain.

"Hey—let me in!" I shouted.

I stared through the fence—and something caught my eye.

In the corner of the swimming pool.

What was it?

I squinted, struggling to see through the curtain of rain.

I gasped when I realized it was a girl. Floating facedown in the pool. Her blond hair bobbing on the surface of the water. Her pale arms stretched lifelessly at her sides.

A girl. A girl in a blue swimsuit.

Drowning.

Drowned.

Gripping the cold fence, I raised my face to the rain and let out a shrill wail of horror.

Chapter 3

DANNY

We were all sitting around in the common room, just goofing, when the rain started. Cassie Harlow let out a shriek when thunder boomed right outside the guest house. She's the sexy one with the great bod, the big brown eyes, and piles of white-blond hair.

It was a little hard to remember who was who, since we were all new to the club. But being that I'm the head lifeguard—the big enchilada—I thought it was important to learn everyone's name and help make everyone feel comfortable.

We all got on Cassie's case for being afraid of thunder. "I'm not afraid. I was just startled," she insisted in that sexy, whispery voice of hers.

But when another boom of thunder made the window shake, Cassie squealed again. "Okay, okay. So

I don't like storms!" she confessed, tugging at her thick hair with both hands.

We all had a good laugh. The little runty guy, Arnie Wilts, said he liked to swim in lightning storms. He said he got a *charge* out of it.

Bad joke.

Everybody groaned. I hoped Arnie wasn't too big a jerk. I mean, I had to spend the whole summer with him. I don't know how many bad jokes like that I could take before I dropped him in the pool and held his head under for five or ten minutes!

I leaned against the windowsill. I could hear rain start to tap against the window at my back. I gazed around the room.

The girls were *outstanding,* I decided, smiling.

Cassie was a total winner. And the one in the pink shorts and sleeveless blue midriff—Deirdre Webb— she was okay too. She had short, straight black hair, very sleek, very shiny. I usually go for longer hair. But Deirdre had the most amazing pale blue eyes.

She was hot. I mean hot.

The tall one in the corner, May-Ann Delacroix— however you pronounce it—wasn't bad either. She had auburn hair and cold dark eyes. She was kind of standoffish. Quiet. Shy, I guess.

But I wouldn't say no to her either.

Outstanding! I thought, gazing from one to the other.

Okay, dudes—let's party all summer!

"How'd you get to be head lifeguard, Danny?" Arnie asked, grinning. "You win a contest or something?"

13

"No way," I told him. "I *lost* a contest!"

Everyone thought that was pretty funny.

Arnie started to say something. He had a grin on his face like he was going to make another bad joke.

Pug interrupted. "Hey, Danny, is there any beer in the fridge?"

Pug looks like a lifeguard. I mean, he could pose in any magazine as your basic, typical hunk of a lifeguard. He obviously works out. He's got a perfect bod. And he's already tanned, even though summer is just starting.

Pug is your all-American dude. He's got curly blond hair, dark eyes that sort of crinkle at the sides, and a big, friendly smile. He looks as if he's never had a serious thought in his entire life. But who knows?

You've *got* to like the guy. He's totally cool.

Pug was sprawled next to Cassie on the leather couch, a red bandanna tied across his forehead. The pirate-dude look, I guess.

I moved away from the window and started to tell Pug about the rule against having beer in the dorm. But a shrill scream interrupted me.

I stopped and spun around.

It sounded as if it came from outside.

At first I thought it was just the storm. Maybe the wind or something. Then I thought maybe a cat had gotten caught in the fence.

But I heard another wail. And this time it definitely sounded human.

I bumped up against Arnie, who was already staring out the fogged-up window. Rubbing my hand against

14

the glass to clear a space, I saw someone. A girl. On the other side of the fence.

She was screaming her head off.

The rain was too loud. I couldn't make out her words. But she sounded really messed up.

"What's going on?" Cassie asked.

"Who's out there?" Deirdre asked, pushing between Arnie and me to see out the window. "Who is *she?*"

Arnie and I went tearing out the door into the pouring rain. It was really coming down. Lightning flashed and crackled. My sneakers sank into a puddle, and I felt the cold water over my ankles.

The girl was screaming and pointing. I couldn't hear a word. The rain was a roar. It was really a heavy-duty storm!

Arnie was a few feet ahead of me. Our sneakers splashed up water as we ran. I struggled to see the girl. Water ran off my forehead into my eyes.

She was totally drenched. Her short blond hair was matted to her head like a helmet. She seemed really frantic and upset.

"What's wrong?"

She screamed something and pointed behind me.

I was nearly at the gate when I heard what she was screaming. "A girl! A girl drowned in the pool! A girl drowned!"

"Huh?" I didn't react at first. I guess I was stunned, in shock or something. I just stared at the girl at the gate, my mouth hanging open.

"A girl in the pool! Look! In the pool!" she screamed.

Finally I came back to life. I tried to wipe the rainwater from my eyes.

"A girl drowned! A girl in the pool!" The girl's shrill cry rose up over the rain.

I turned and, shielding my eyes with one hand, started running back to the swimming pool.

My heart was pounding. I was running so fast, I slipped a couple of times on the wet pavement and almost fell on my face.

The girl's screams faded behind me, into the steady roar of the falling rain.

I reached the pool a few seconds later, breathing hard.

Who can it be? I wondered. Who could have drowned in the swimming pool? The club is closed. Closed. Closed.

I took a deep breath and stared into the pool.

Blinking away rainwater, I stared again. Up and down the entire pool.

There was no one there. No one at all.

Chapter 4

LINDSAY

I was so embarrassed.

I was totally mortified.

That's how I met my new friends, the other life-guards.

Soaked to the skin. A wet, shivering blob.

As the red-haired one, Danny, and the skinny little one, Arnie, led me into the common room, I was still gasping and choking. My throat was raw from screaming.

I just wanted to disappear. To melt onto the floor like a puddle of rainwater.

My T-shirt was stuck to my skin. My hair was matted down to my forehead. My high-tops were filled with water.

I lowered my duffel bag. It made a squishing sound as it hit the floor.

One of the girls, a tall girl with short, straight auburn hair, introduced herself. May-Ann Delacroix. She ran to get me a towel.

But I didn't want a towel. I wanted a hole, a deep hole to sink into, a place to hide. Forever.

"What happened?"

"Why were you screaming?"

"Were you locked out?"

"What did you see?"

"What were you *doing* out there?"

"Did someone hurt you?"

I was bombarded with questions. Their faces reflected their concern and confusion.

I couldn't answer them. I was shivering too hard to talk.

I tried to wipe the water out of my eyes with the back of my hand. But more water just dripped off my forehead.

"Get her something to drink," someone said. "Something hot."

"I—I'm okay," I finally managed to stammer.

May-Ann hurried back into the room and wrapped a bath towel around my shoulders. I took it and tried to dry my hair.

My heart was still racing. But I was starting to feel a little more normal.

Danny, the redheaded guy, had disappeared. He reappeared in dry clothes, a long-sleeved blue pullover and white tennis shorts.

"What's your name?" he asked. I guessed he was the head lifeguard. He was acting like he was in charge.

I told him. "Lindsay Beck."

He quickly introduced all the others to me. It was impossible to keep them straight. Of course, I remembered May-Ann. She was the tall girl who had brought me the towel. A pretty girl with sleek black hair was named Deirdre. A big, blond jock-type with a red bandanna was named Pug.

They all clustered around me, staring at me as if I were some kind of freak or museum exhibit.

"The girl in the pool—" I started to explain to Danny. But I stopped. I mean, how could I explain it?

He shook his head. "I don't know what you saw, Lindsay. There wasn't anything in the pool. A few leaves."

I swallowed hard.

I had seen her, seen her so clearly. She was wearing a blue bikini. Her skin was so pale. Her hair, floating on top of the water, was blond, like mine.

"I—I'm sorry," I stammered, feeling my face grow hot. "It must have been the rain. Shadows or something. I feel like a total jerk."

"Hey—no problem," Danny replied, smiling at me. He had a nice smile. I don't usually like redheaded guys with freckles, but he was cute. "I *needed* a shower!" he joked.

"Yeah. You did," Arnie, the little guy who had also run out in the rain, joked.

I shook my head, trying to fluff up my hair. Then I dried off my arms and hands with the towel. May-Ann had returned to the armchair across the room. She was staring at me, as if studying me. She had cold, dark eyes and a hard expression on her face.

"You really thought you saw someone in the pool?"

19

a girl with a throaty whisper of a voice asked. I'd already forgotten her name. She shook her head under tangles of white-blond hair. "Wow."

"Why were you at the gate?" Pug asked. "The club doesn't open till tomorrow."

"She wanted an early swim!" Arnie joked. "You know. Before it gets crowded."

No one laughed.

"I'm a lifeguard," I told them. I glanced down at my soggy duffel bag. "I know I don't *look* like one at the moment. But I am."

"Hey—lifeguards aren't supposed to get wet!" Pug joked. "It's against union rules."

"How many lifeguards *are* there this year?" I heard the girl with all the blond hair whisper to Deirdre. Deirdre shrugged.

Danny had a bewildered expression on his face. He walked over to the desk against the wall and began shuffling through some files.

"Here's the list," he said, pulling out a sheet of paper. He smiled at me. But his smile faded as his eyes ran down the list of lifeguards.

"What did you say your last name was, Lindsay?" he asked.

"Beck," I told him. I felt so uncomfortable. I glanced down and saw that I was standing in a puddle now. I *had* to get to my room and change. I was still dripping.

"Weird," Danny murmured, twisting up his face. He held up the sheet of paper. "There's no Lindsay Beck on the lifeguard list."

"Huh?" I let out a startled gasp. I gripped the towel

in both hands. "This just isn't my day," I muttered, rolling my eyes. "How could they leave me off?"

"Maybe you're at the wrong club," May-Ann suggested from across the room. She turned to Danny. "Or maybe she's the alternate."

Danny shook his head. "No. She's not."

I felt a tiny knot of dread form in my stomach. "Someone messed up," I told Danny, trying to sound calm but not quite pulling it off. "I should be on the list. If I'm not a lifeguard here, why did they send me this ID card?"

I pulled the card out of my jeans pocket. It was wet, but the water rolled right off.

Danny crossed the room and took the card from me. He narrowed his eyes as he studied it carefully.

"Lindsay, are you sure this is the ID card you received?" he asked.

I nodded. "Yes."

I glanced around the room. The other lifeguards were all frozen in place, staring at me suspiciously.

Danny studied the card some more. Then he slowly raised his eyes to mine.

"Wh-what's wrong?" I stammered.

"Lindsay," Danny said softly, his eyes still searching mine, "this ID card is two years old."

Chapter 5

MAY-ANN

"What is going *on* here?" the girl cried.

I felt so sorry for her.

There she was, standing in a big puddle of water, soaked to the bone, shivering and shaking. She looked so pitiful.

And confused. I mean, her name wasn't on the list, and she had a two-year-old ID.

Somebody had messed up.

The others were staring at her as if she'd just dropped down from Mars. I'm sure *that* made her feel really terrific. Even Danny, who's supposed to be in charge, wasn't doing anything to help.

So I decided to do something. I mean, at least I could help her get changed into some dry clothes.

I crossed the room and took her arm. "Come on. You can change in my room," I told her.

Her expression softened. She looked really grateful. I helped her carry her soaking-wet duffel bag, and we started toward the hall that led to my room.

Lindsay turned in the doorway and gazed back at everyone. "Wasn't anyone here last year?" she asked. Her voice was shrill and high. She sounded really upset. "Are you all new to the club?"

"All new," Danny told her. He still had the list in his hand.

"Arnie is new to the *planet!*" the big jock named Pug joked.

Everyone laughed.

Lindsay stared at them uncertainly. "I was here last year," she said. "I thought maybe somebody would remember. . . ." Her voice trailed off.

Pug stepped away from Cassie. He'd been coming on to her all afternoon. He was practically licking her hand. I think she was enjoying it too.

Cassie was your basic flirt. She even flirted with the little weasely guy, Arnie. I couldn't *believe* her telling Arnie how much she liked that little dangly earring he wears.

The other girl, Deirdre, the really pretty one—she kept glaring at Cassie. I think Deirdre is interested in Pug too.

Pug took a few steps toward Lindsay, fiddling with his red bandanna as he walked. "I was a guest here last year," he told Lindsay.

"Who'd let *you* in?" Arnie interrupted. Arnie giggled at his own joke.

"But I don't remember seeing you," Pug told Lindsay.

"Weird," Lindsay replied, staring fretfully at Pug. "I don't remember you either. I was on duty every afternoon." She shook her head. Water dripped down her cheeks.

"Pete will get this all straightened out," Danny said, putting the list back into its folder. "Pete typed the list. He probably messed up, that's all," Danny said.

Pete Harris is the hotshot athletic director we were all waiting to see. Pete is amazing. He has more energy than anyone I ever met. While he interviewed me for the lifeguard job last spring, he did a hundred push-ups and a hundred sit-ups in front of his desk!

Sure, he was just showing off. But I was impressed.

I don't think it's possible for Pete to do only one thing at a time. He has to be doing at least three or four activities at once.

"Come on. Before you shiver to death," I urged Lindsay. I led the way down the narrow hall to my room. "Talk about your bad hair day!" I joked. Her hair looked like a blond helmet.

She forced a laugh. But I could see she had a lot of thoughts running through her mind.

She changed quickly, pulling on a pair of dry, faded jeans ripped at both knees and a maroon and gray sweatshirt that said Tigers on the front.

Then she spent a lot of time drying her hair, fluffing it with both hands, trying to get it to look like hair again. All the time she stared hard at herself in the mirror, her eyes narrowed, her mouth set in a straight line.

My room was pretty small. Two single beds, two

small dressers, a bookshelf against one wall, a small armchair, a couple of end tables.

While Lindsay was getting changed, I walked over to my dresser and peered into Munchy's cage. Munchy is my white mouse. My only pet. I don't normally travel with Munchy. It's not like I'm *that* attached to the little rodent. But my parents were traveling this summer, so I had to bring Munchy with me.

I poured some seeds into his little cup. Then I turned back to Lindsay. "How you doing? Feel better?" I asked.

"I just don't get it," she replied, biting her lower lip.

Now that she had gotten herself together, I saw that she was really nice-looking. Not beautiful or anything. Kind of perky. Cute.

"I really thought I saw someone drowning in the pool," she said, frowning. She shut her eyes. Picturing it again, I imagined.

"The light was so weird," I suggested, "because of the storm. Probably something reflected—"

"And why is my ID card two years old?" she interrupted. I don't think she heard me at all. She was so deep into her own thoughts.

She picked up the ID card from where she had set it on the dresser top. She glanced at it, then slid it into her jeans pocket.

"And why aren't I on the list?" A short cry escaped from her lips. "I *know* I was accepted. I *know* it's not my mistake."

"Pete will straighten it all out," I assured her. What else could I say?

25

We heard loud laughter floating out from the common room. Pug was doing some kind of loud animal roar, and everyone was cracking up.

When the laughter stopped, I heard Deirdre make a comment about Lindsay. Everyone laughed. I glanced at Lindsay, wondering if she had heard.

But she still seemed to be lost in her own thoughts.

"Come on. Let's go back," I said. "You can just leave your stuff."

She nodded. We walked back to the common room.

Everyone had been laughing, but they stopped the moment we reappeared.

I dropped into the armchair against the wall. Lindsay gazed around uncertainly, then settled on a folding chair beside the desk.

"You look a little better," Danny told her, smiling.

"Thanks," Lindsay replied awkwardly. "I'm drier, at least." She turned her eyes to me. "Thanks, May-Ann."

Thunder boomed, shaking the windowpanes. I glanced at the window. It was as black as night outside. Sheets of rain battered the glass.

"How about a swim?" Arnie suggested.

"You first," Pug told him.

"Dare me?" Arnie challenged him.

I think Arnie's got some kind of problem. I don't know *what* he wants to prove.

It got very quiet. Everyone suddenly ran out of things to say. We were all strangers, after all. It's not like we were old pals.

Across the room Lindsay was nibbling her lower lip, thinking hard.

I leaned forward in my chair. I hadn't planned to tell her—but it just slipped out. "Lindsay," I said softly, my voice breaking through the heavy silence. "I know who you saw floating in the swimming pool."

Lindsay glanced up, startled. "Who?"

"You saw one of the dead kids," I told her.

Chapter 6

DANNY

Well, that sure got everyone's attention.

Just as May-Ann said that, a roar of thunder made the whole room shake, and the lights went out. One of the girls let out a shriek. I think it was Cassie.

I heard Arnie and Pug laughing. Arnie started making spooky ghost sounds. You know— *ooooooooooh.*

Gray light filtered in through the window. Then jagged lightning forked through the sky. The window glass was covered with raindrops. It all looked totally unreal.

A few seconds later the lights flickered back on. Everybody cheered.

I saw that Pug had slid closer on the couch to Cassie. What a guy! He'd just met her, and was already making a move on her.

Deirdre kept glancing at them. I think she had her eye on Pug. I started to feel a little jealous. I mean, *whoa!* If Cassie and Deirdre both went for Pug, who was left for me?

Lindsay had her arms crossed tightly in front of her. She was pretty tense. I wondered if she ever relaxed. I mean, was she always this stressed out? Or was she just upset because of the mix-up with the lifeguard list?

I started to ask if anyone had a flashlight, in case the storm knocked the lights out for good.

But Lindsay interrupted. "What do you mean?" she asked May-Ann. "What dead kids?"

"Yeah. What are you talking about?" Pug demanded.

Everyone turned back to May-Ann. She was wearing baggy white shorts, and she had her long legs crossed. I go for tall girls. I mean, I think they're really sexy.

But I wasn't sure about May-Ann. Sometimes my first impressions can be wrong. But I thought there was something strange about her, something cold and unfriendly.

"This club is cursed," May-Ann said in a low voice. She narrowed her eyes. "It's a bad-luck place."

Everyone was staring at her now. "What are you talking about?" I asked her. It's my job as head honcho to keep everyone's morale up. I didn't like the way May-Ann was talking.

We were all just getting to know one another. I didn't need someone freaking the others out before the club even opened.

"People die here every summer. Mysterious deaths," May-Ann murmured, her voice just loud enough to be heard over the pattering rain.

"Someone has drowned in the pool for the last two summers," she continued.

"Huh? The same person drowned two years in a row?" Arnie cried.

It wasn't very funny. None of Arnie's jokes are very funny. But everyone laughed. Nervous laughter, I guess.

I mean, everyone laughed except May-Ann. She tucked her legs under her, her dark eyes glowing with excitement. "It's true," she insisted.

"What happened?" Deirdre's voice broke through the silence. "Who drowned?"

"Last year a fourteen-year-old boy," May-Ann told her. "He drowned in the deep end of the pool—even though there were three lifeguards on duty."

"Wow," I heard Cassie murmur. She was shaking her head thoughtfully.

Deirdre cleared her throat and stared down at her sandals. No one said a word.

"Two years ago, a *lifeguard* drowned!" May-Ann continued. "Can you imagine? A lifeguard! Drowned in the shallow end of the pool!"

Another flash of light and explosion of thunder.

Even I jumped at that one.

I glanced around the room at serious faces. May-Ann was creeping everyone out. Lindsay really seemed freaked.

"This club is *haunted* by the kids who drowned here," May-Ann said solemnly. "Haunted."

No one said a word. The silence got really heavy.

Finally I shouted, "Boo!"

Everyone laughed.

"It's a little early for ghost stories," I told May-Ann.

"It's not a story. It's true," she insisted.

"How could a lifeguard drown?" Deirdre asked, tossing her black hair.

"Probably fell asleep," Arnie suggested, grinning.

"Didn't know how to swim!" Pug added. "Only knew how to get a tan!"

Everyone laughed.

I was glad they were cheering up. May-Ann was really giving me a pain. I mean, she didn't have to bring everyone down like that—did she?

Then Lindsay's voice rose over the laughter. "Do you really believe in ghosts?" she asked May-Ann.

May-Ann nodded solemnly. "Yes," she replied in a low voice. "I know this club is haunted. The ghosts of the drowned cannot rest."

Most of us started to laugh. I mean, May-Ann was just too cornball for words.

But we stopped laughing as the door to the common room suddenly creaked.

The sound made me focus on the door.

It creaked again and started to swing open.

We heard footsteps, shoes scraping the floorboards in the hall.

The door swung all the way open.

But there was no one there.

Chapter 7

LINDSAY

I let out a silent gasp as the door creaked.

I felt a cold chill at the back of my neck. I heard footsteps and saw the door slowly open. But no one came in.

Across the room May-Ann had a pleased smile on her face. As if she had been proven right about the ghosts.

No one else was smiling. Danny's mouth hung open. We all sat in stunned silence. Listening.

More footsteps.

Finally a dark-haired boy stepped hesitantly into the room, shaking water off his blue windbreaker. "Sorry," he murmured as he tugged the windbreaker off. "The outer door." He pointed back to the hallway. "I thought I closed it. But the wind blew it open."

"We thought you were a ghost!" Danny exclaimed.

We all laughed.

The boy seemed confused.

I glanced at May-Ann. She was frowning in disappointment.

The boy folded his windbreaker into a compact square. Then he stood, holding it awkwardly. He didn't know where to put it.

He was nice looking. He had straight dark brown hair pulled back into a short ponytail. He had big, dark eyes, solemn eyes. He had a serious face, I thought. I guessed he didn't smile much.

Just a first impression.

"My bag—I left it in the hall," he said, raking a hand back through his long hair, adjusting the ponytail. "Sorry I'm late." He gazed around quickly. "I guess I'm the last one here."

"You're Spencer Brown?" Danny asked.

The boy nodded.

"Hey, I wondered where you were," Danny told him. "I thought maybe the storm—"

"My ride was late," Spencer said.

And I suddenly realized that he looked familiar. Finally. A familiar face.

My heart actually skipped a beat. Yes! I *knew* him!

I was so excited, I jumped to my feet. "Hi! Remember me?" I cried. I took a few steps toward him in the center of the room.

Spencer narrowed his eyes as if trying to remember me. Then his mouth dropped open, and he uttered a startled, "Huh?"

"Remember me? Lindsay Beck?" I asked excitedly.

He stared at me for the longest time. His eyes were

sort of fluttering as he studied me. I could practically *see* all the thoughts whirring through his brain.

"Lindsay?" he asked uncertainly. "You're Lindsay?"

I nodded, smiling hopefully at him.

Finally the confusion left his face and he smiled back. "Hey—Lindsay!" he cried. "I didn't recognize you. Hey! How's it going? You're back for another summer?"

"Yeah. I just can't stay away from the place!" I exclaimed.

I felt really happy that someone knew me.

I turned to Danny. He was smiling too.

"So—what's up?" I asked Spencer.

He shrugged. "Not much. Some storm, huh?"

"Yeah."

Danny made his way over to Spencer and started introducing him to the other lifeguards. Spencer repeated each name, trying to memorize it.

Suddenly a guy in a yellow slicker came bursting into the room.

"Yo—Pete!" Danny cried.

I realized it must be Pete, the club's athletic director. He looked about twenty. Short and kind of stocky. His cheeks were red. He had tiny, round blue eyes like little marbles. He wore his light brown hair in a short flattop.

He bustled into the room, walking very fast, shaking water off his yellow slicker. I had to chuckle to myself. Pete looked like a big duck!

"Hey, people—how's it going?" he greeted us. He smiled at May-Ann. "Everybody here? Everybody happy? Everybody dry?" He talked rapidly, without taking a breath, and didn't give anyone a chance to reply.

"You people have to help me out this year," he said, tossing the yellow slicker over the desk. "It's my first year too, you know?"

Everyone clustered around Pete and tried to talk to him at once. I hung back, standing near the window.

I realized I had never met him.

"Okay, people," Pete said, motioning with both hands for everyone to stop chattering at once. "Everyone get shift assignments? Did Danny get to that yet? Everyone got their assigned rooms? Two to a room, right? No—*not* boy-girl, boy-girl!"

Everyone laughed.

"Arnie—who's your roommate?" Pete demanded, pointing a stubby finger at Arnie.

"His mother!" Pug yelled.

More loud laughter. Arnie, red-faced, playfully shoved Pug.

"Spencer is Arnie's roommate," Danny announced, his eyes on Spencer. "I didn't get a chance to break the bad news to him yet!"

"Ha-ha," Arnie said sarcastically. "That's real funny, dude."

"So it's you and Pug?" Pete asked Danny, pulling a clipboard out of the desk drawer.

"Yeah," Danny replied. "And Cassie and Deirdre. They're in the big room."

"The suite!" Pete said, grinning at the two girls. "Suites for the sweet! Ha-ha!"

Everyone groaned.

"And then there's May-Ann and—" Danny stopped. He suddenly remembered me. He tugged at Pete's clipboard. "Can I see that? We have a little mix-up." He glanced at me.

I was still standing by the window. The lightning and thunder had stopped. The rain was soft and light now.

I watched Danny tell Pete about me. They kept raising their eyes to me, then gazed down at the clipboard as they talked.

Finally Pete came hurrying over to me, smiling, his tiny blue eyes studying me. "Lindsay? Hi, I'm Pete."

He shook hands with me. His hand was still wet from the rain. "You seem to have dropped off the list," Pete said, holding up the clipboard and studying it again. "When did we talk? In the fall? In the spring?"

"I—I don't remember," I stammered.

"I don't either," he said, scratching his short flat-top. "But I *had* to interview you. I hired only people I interviewed. I'll have to check your file, I guess."

"I got my ID card, and I—uh—" I wasn't sure what to say. Why didn't I remember talking with him? Why didn't I remember any interview?

"I was a lifeguard here last summer," I told him. "And I—"

"Hey—a veteran!" Pete exclaimed, grinning at me. "Maybe you should have *my* job!"

"No, I don't think so," I replied awkwardly. Glancing over Pete's shoulder, I saw Spencer's dark eyes trained on me.

"Sorry about the mix-up," Pete was saying. "I always do ten things at once, and sometimes I mess up." He glanced down at the clipboard. "Weird," he muttered. "I really don't have a place for you, Lindsay."

I swallowed hard. I had a heavy feeling of dread in the pit of my stomach. "You d-don't?" I stammered. "But I—"

Pete eyed me suspiciously. "You've passed all your lifesaving tests?"

I nodded. "Yeah. Two summers ago."

He rubbed his chin again. "I should remember you," he murmured. "Weird. Weird." He gazed at the clipboard, then turned to Danny. "Lindsay can be the alternate," he told Danny. "That girl from Sheffield canceled out on us. Got a better offer, I guess."

"Is that okay with you?" Danny asked me.

I breathed a sigh of relief. They weren't going to send me home.

"Great!" I exclaimed. "You mean I just fill in when I'm needed?"

"Don't worry. With *this* crew, you'll be needed!" Pete said dryly.

"She can room with May-Ann," Danny suggested. He glanced at May-Ann, who was standing by the couch, braiding and unbraiding short strands of her auburn hair. "Unless May-Ann has a ghost she wants to room with," Danny joked.

"You're so funny," May-Ann said, scowling. "Remind me to laugh later."

"So you're set?" Pete asked me.

"I'm set. Thanks," I replied.

"Have a good summer, Lindsay," he said, turning to the others. "Almost dinnertime, you guys. I assume you've already checked out where the dining room is?" He pointed with the clipboard to the swinging half-door at one end of the common room. "Pug, you putting on weight? Is that a roll of flab, or what?"

"Hey—no way!" Pug cried angrily. "You know I work out every day, Pete. Every day. I'm going straight to the weight room after dinner. If you'd like to go one on one with me—"

"I just might do that," Pete replied, his blue eyes twinkling.

"I've been pumping up too," Arnie broke in.

Pete made a face. "Arnie, please—not before dinner. Keep it to yourself, okay?"

Most everyone laughed.

"Hey—I'm serious!" Arnie protested. "I'm small, Pete, but I'm all muscle. Really."

"I've got to run," Pete said, grabbing up his yellow rain slicker. "Remember, people—nine A.M. tomorrow. That's when we open. This rain is supposed to blow out of here by then. So we will be opening. You've got your shift assignments, right? And—"

"I need to talk to you," Cassie said, stepping in front of him, blocking his exit.

"Cassie, looking good!" Pete said, grinning. I saw May-Ann frown across the room.

"I really don't like the kiddie pool in the morning," Cassie complained in her hoarse whisper. "I need something a little busier—you know, to wake me up."

"Well . . ." Pete hesitated. "Danny drew up the assignments, Cassie."

She turned to Danny. "Maybe someone could

switch with me. Maybe Deirdre could do the kiddie pool in the morning."

"Hey—no way!" Deirdre protested. I was surprised by how angry she sounded. It was pretty obvious that Deirdre didn't like Cassie very much. She had been glaring at Cassie all afternoon.

I think Deirdre was definitely interested in Pug. And I think she was upset that Pug was interested in Cassie.

"I'll check the schedules," Danny promised Cassie. "Maybe we can switch off on the kiddie pool."

That seemed to satisfy Cassie.

Pete hurried out, his yellow rain slicker flapping behind him.

I was feeling a little better, more like I belonged. I had looked forward to this summer for so long. I had looked forward to coming back to the club, to having a great summer. I didn't want anything to spoil it.

I turned and gazed at Spencer. He was talking to May-Ann. I studied him, trying to remember him.

Spencer Brown. Spencer Brown.

What do I know about him? I asked myself, searching my memory.

Spencer Brown . . .

Spencer Brown . . .

I stared hard at him, at his oversize white T-shirt pulled down over black denim cutoffs. At his dark eyes, his serious expression as he listened to May-Ann.

I stared hard at Spencer—and realized with a sinking feeling that I didn't remember a single thing about him.

Chapter 8

MOUSE

*H*ey, Terry. How's it going?

Yeah, it's me. Mouse.

I'm here, Terry. I'm here at the North Beach Country Club. Do you believe it?

You don't have to answer, Terry. I know you're dead. But I had to call you anyway.

I had to tell you I made it. I'm a lifeguard. Yeah. They gave me a whistle and everything. Ha-ha.

I know you're there, Terry. I know you can hear me.

I know how happy you are for me.

I'm doing it for you. You know that, right?

I told you that.

It's raining now. Can you tell that it's raining—even though you're dead? Can you feel it in the ground? Can you hear it, Terry?

It's raining now, but the pool is going to open tomorrow.

I'm in my room, Terry. I'm in the lifeguard dorm. Yeah. It's okay. Better than okay. The room's real nice. I've got my own bed and my own desk.

I've got a roommate too.

I wish it were you, Terry. I really do.

You know I do.

I can't talk long. My roommate will be here.

Should I kill my roommate, Terry? Is that who I should kill first?

It's up to you, Terry.

Yeah. I know you're dead.

But it's up to you.

Chapter 9

DANNY

We had a good time at dinner—until May-Ann started talking about ghosts again. Then it got pretty tense.

I think everyone was surprised by how good the food was. Lonnie, the cook, knows his way around fried chicken. The mashed potatoes were lumpy, but they tasted great if you loaded on plenty of salt.

Pug and Arnie almost got into a mashed-potato fight. But one disapproving glance from Cassie made Pug put down the mashed potato bowl.

Cassie and Deirdre both came on to Pug all through dinner. I admit it, I was turning as green as the steamed spinach that no one touched. I'm the big cheese, after all, the main guy. Those girls were *supposed* to come after *my* bod!

Maybe *I'll* get a red bandanna, I told myself, if that's what it takes to turn girls on.

Pug, of course, started bragging about what great shape he was in, how he worked out every day. "I'm the only one here who looks like a lifeguard!" he boasted.

"Give me a break," I replied. I crooked my arm and showed him a pretty good bicep.

"I can take on both of you with my eyes closed," Spencer bragged.

That was a surprise. Spencer had been talking quietly to May-Ann the whole time.

Arnie, of course, had been Arnie, cracking horrible jokes, bragging about how strong he was, even though it's obvious that he's a puny shrimp. Arnie kept gazing across the table at Lindsay. I think he had the hots for her.

I never saw her even glance in his direction. I don't think she had any idea that Arnie kept checking her out.

Lindsay is cute. She has a great face, innocent, like a little girl's face. But she seems really stressed. She didn't talk much at dinner. She kept staring at Spencer, studying him.

The only time Lindsay really got interested in the conversation was when Spencer started talking about last summer. She looked up from her plate when he said the lifeguards were real party animals.

"They totally trashed the dorm," Spencer said, his dark eyes lighting up. "They totally trashed it. It was party-till-you-puke every night!"

"Well, wait till *this* year gets going!" Pug cried, grinning at Cassie. He began chanting: "Par-tee! Par-tee! Par-tee!"

Cassie got up and tended the fire, poking the logs, making the red embers leap into flame.

I couldn't believe she wanted a fire. It *is* the end of June, after all.

But Cassie insisted she was cold and wanted a fire. There was a good supply of logs and kindling next to the fireplace. So, why not?

I started on my third helping of chicken and mashed potatoes. The stuff was good! Back home, both my parents worked, so we usually ate take-out. You know, McDonald's or something. I kept thinking it was funny I had to come to a club to get a home-cooked meal.

When Cassie got back to the table, her face red from leaning close to the fire, Spencer was still yakking about how great last summer was.

Suddenly Lindsay interrupted with a question that stopped the conversation dead. "Were you on duty when the fourteen-year-old boy drowned?" she asked Spencer.

He practically choked on his iced tea.

"No way," he replied, getting a real solemn expression on his face. He shook his head. "I wasn't there, Lindsay. I wasn't even at the club that day. I only heard about it."

It got really quiet in the room. The only sound was the crackling of the fire in the stone fireplace.

"Did anyone talk about the ghosts?" Lindsay asked Spencer.

Spencer acted confused. "Ghosts?"

"Did anyone see anything weird?" Lindsay continued. She was nervously tapping the table with her fork. "I mean, did any of the lifeguards see a drowned girl in the pool or anything?"

A burned-up log crumbled in the fire, dropping out of the grate and sending up a rush of red embers. Cassie got up again to poke the fire.

Spencer stared across the table at Lindsay. I could tell he didn't know what she was talking about.

"The ghosts are here," May-Ann said softly. She moved her eyes slowly around the dining room as if searching for them. "Everyone knows about them."

She was really starting to creep me out.

I mean, if May-Ann was so worried about ghosts, why did she take a job here?

"May-Ann, save it for Halloween," Pug grumbled through a mouthful of fried chicken.

"Yeah. Give us a break," Arnie joined in.

"Afraid you'll have nightmares?" May-Ann asked him, sneering.

"You're a nightmare!" Arnie exclaimed. Pretty lame reply. But Cassie and Deirdre laughed.

"Whoa—let's change the subject," I suggested.

I saw May-Ann's cheeks turn red. I saw that she was gripping her knife tightly. She glared angrily at Arnie. "You think you're a real funny dude, don't you? But kids have *died* here. And their spirits haven't left."

Arnie opened his mouth to reply—but a scream made him freeze.

I practically fell off my chair.

45

I turned toward the fireplace to see who had screamed. It was Cassie, her face red in the light from the fire. She was pointing to the door with a trembling finger.

"The ghost!" Cassie cried in a terrified whisper. "There it is!"

Chapter 10

DANNY

We all turned to where Cassie was pointing.

May-Ann jumped to her feet. "I *knew* it!" she cried. "Where is it? *Where?*"

Cassie again pointed to the door. But then she broke up.

Her knees bent and she sort of collapsed in laughter. She had a funny, high-pitched giggle. It sort of trickled out like a waterfall. She covered her mouth with one hand and closed her eyes as she laughed.

"Gotcha!" she cried.

It took us a few seconds to get over our shock. Then we all started laughing our heads off too.

Everyone except May-Ann.

She was still standing. She gripped the table edge with both hands, and her jaw was clenched in anger.

I could see she was really steamed.

She let out a loud cry. It was like an explosion of anger.

Those cold, dark eyes of hers moved from face to face. Then she screamed, "We'll see who's laughing at the end of the summer!" She tossed her napkin onto her plate, turned, and stomped out of the room.

Arnie was still laughing. The rest of us watched in stunned silence as May-Ann stormed out.

"Hey, May-Ann—come back!" I called.

She slammed the door behind her.

I don't need this, I thought, shaking my head. I really wanted everyone to be pumped for opening day.

Why did we have to have yelling and slamming doors on our very first night?

This could be a long summer, I thought unhappily.

"You know, guys, we really should give May-Ann a break," I said.

"Why doesn't she give *us* a break?" Arnie demanded.

"All that ghost talk is starting to freak me out," Deirdre said. "I mean, are we going to have fun this summer? Or are we going to sit around talking about drowned kids and ghosts?"

"It—it's my fault," Lindsay stammered, staring down at her untouched food. "I shouldn't have asked Spencer . . ." Her voice trailed off.

Cassie was still poking the fire. "May-Ann really has a short fuse," she murmured. "She *can't* be serious about all that ghost stuff—can she? I mean *whoa*, where's her sense of humor?"

"Hey, Lonnie—what's for dessert?" I shouted into the kitchen. I was desperate to change the subject.

I was actually glad when Spencer and Pug started arm-wrestling down at the far end of the table. Everyone began cheering and urging them on.

"Hey, I'll take the winner!" Arnie cried.

Everyone laughed.

But I could see Arnie was serious. "I'm stronger than I look!" he insisted. "I can beat anyone here. I'll take you all on one by one! Really!"

"You can't beat me!" Cassie called to Arnie from the fire. She grinned and crooked her arm to make a muscle.

"I want the winner!" Arnie insisted, ignoring her.

I really couldn't believe him. Did he really think he was some kind of awesome power-dude? Didn't he know he was a shrimp? Pug or Spencer could *crush* him like a bug!

Arnie was so eager to prove he was a tough dude, it was funny and sad at the same time.

I took a long drink of my Coke and stood up to get a better view of the action.

Pug and Spencer were just goofing at first.

Laughing, Pug deliberately fell off the chair. Then Spencer offered to arm-wrestle him with just one pinkie finger.

At first it was all in fun.

But then they started in for real, and it got pretty intense.

Spencer's dark eyes narrowed in concentration. I could see his jaw working, his teeth clenched.

Pug tore off his bandanna and tossed it to the floor. As he pushed against Spencer's arm, beads of sweat glistened on his broad forehead.

The room grew totally silent.

Spencer took an early advantage. With a low groan, he tilted Pug's hand down close to the table.

Pug's face got all twisted from his effort. With a burst of strength, he pushed Spencer's hand straight up.

They were even for a few seconds, both of them straining, both sweating.

They're starting to take this a little too seriously, I thought. One of them should give in.

Pug let out a roar and took the advantage, pushing against Spencer's hand. Pushing, pushing.

Spencer's arm started to tilt down.

Give up, Spencer! I silently urged. *Please—end it!*

Pug pushed harder. Spencer's hand was forced down. Down.

The room was so silent.

Then the silence was broken by a loud, sickening *craaaack.*

And Spencer's face went white.

Chapter 11

LINDSAY

"**O**ww!"

When the horrible *craaaack* cut through the air, I was so startled, I bit my tongue.

Down at the end of the table, Spencer went as white as a sheet.

His hand dropped lifelessly to the table.

Pug's eyes practically bulged out of his head. Sweat rolled off his forehead. His mouth dropped open.

No one made a sound.

Then, once again, Cassie's high-pitched giggle broke the silence.

With a surprised gasp, I turned—and saw that Cassie was holding up two pieces of broken kindling.

"Crack-crack," she said, laughing. She gestured with the two halves of the kindling.

"Oh, wow!" I heard Deirdre cry out. "Cassie strikes again!"

It took me a long while to figure out that Cassie had cracked the stick in half. That the sound hadn't been made by Spencer's arm.

What a hoot!

Spencer was still breathing hard. His dark eyes were dull and lifeless, but the color started to come back to his cheeks.

Pug laughed and slapped the table. I think he was relieved that he hadn't broken Spencer's arm.

We all laughed. Nervous, relieved laughter.

"Aren't I a devil?" Cassie asked, grinning coyly as she returned to the table.

Spencer shook his arm. He examined his hand. "I really thought you broke my arm," he told Pug. "I was just waiting for the pain to come. I couldn't figure out why there was no pain."

"Cassie is the pain!" Arnie joked.

"You guys were getting too serious," Cassie replied. "I had to do something."

"Hey, I want a rematch," Spencer told Pug.

"You lost, man. I had you beat," Pug insisted.

"Cassie helped you win," Spencer said heatedly. "I could've taken you." He turned to Cassie. "I owe you one. I'll get you, Cassie. Really."

"Ooh, I'm shaking!" Cassie exclaimed sarcastically.

"My turn!" Arnie insisted. He tried pushing Spencer out of the way. "Come on, guys. I called winners."

Pug looked at Arnie as if he were a piece of decayed meat. "In your dreams," Pug told him.

Everyone laughed.

Arnie leaned over Pug menacingly. "You chicken? Come on, dude. You chicken?"

I cried out, startled, as Pug jumped to his feet. He reached out and lifted Arnie off the floor.

"How about some basketball?" Pug cried.

I saw where he was going. He was carrying Arnie to the tall metal wastebasket.

"Put me down, man!" Arnie screamed, thrashing his arms frantically.

"Here comes a three-point shot!" Pug cried.

He stuffed Arnie into the wastebasket.

Everyone cheered.

"Nice shot, Pug!" Cassie cried. "But you forgot to dribble him!"

Deirdre was shaking her head. Spencer was still rubbing his wrist.

I could see an impatient expression on Danny's face. I think he could see that things had gotten out of control. "Hey, guys—how about dessert?" he called.

I decided to skip dessert. My head was spinning. From all the new faces and all the talk and laughter, I guess.

I told everyone good night and hurried down the long hall to my room.

I wanted to see if I could cheer up May-Ann. She was obviously sensitive. The guys would have to stop teasing her so much.

I crept quietly into the room in case May-Ann had gone to bed. The room was nearly dark. A small reading lamp was lit on her bed table, the only light in the room.

"May-Ann?" I called quietly.

She wasn't there.

I glanced in the bathroom. She wasn't there either.

Maybe she went out for a walk or something, I thought.

I started toward the phone, but stopped when I saw May-Ann's dresser top.

"Ohh!" I let out a low cry as my eyes tried to focus in the dim light.

The dresser was crawling with mice!

Chapter 12

MOUSE

*T*hey laughed at me, Terry.

Yeah. It's me, Mouse. I'm not calling too late, am I?

I guess it's never too late for you, huh? Since you can't hear me anyway.

Well, they can't laugh at you anymore, can they?

But they laughed at me tonight.

I don't care. I'm used to it. We're both used to it, right, Terry?

Lifeguards think they're such hot stuff. They don't care about a person's feelings.

They never cared about our feelings, did they, Terry?

But it's all different now. All different. Know what I mean?

For one thing, I'm one of them.

I'm a lifeguard too. But I already told you that, didn't I?

What do you care if I repeat myself, Terry? You're dead! Ha-ha.

No, I'm not laughing at you. Really.

I don't laugh at you. When I think about you, Terry, I don't want to laugh. I want to cry.

Know what else is different?

I'm stronger now. Yeah. No lie. I've been working out.

I'm strong, Terry. I'm a real strong person.

And I'm going to kill them all.

Kill them for laughing at you. Kill them for laughing at me.

We'll see who's laughing when the summer is over. We'll see, Terry.

You know what my main problem is?

I can't decide which one to do first.

Chapter 13

LINDSAY

"Ow." I gingerly touched my shoulder.

Sunburned.

It had been cloudy all day, the opening day for the club. I had forgotten how easy it is to get burned right through the clouds.

Feeling like a jerk, I headed to the bathroom to get some aloe lotion. As I searched the medicine cabinet, I thought about what a disappointing day it had been.

The threatening clouds had kept all but a few hardy swimmers from the club. At noon, when I took over the kiddie pool from Cassie, there were three toddlers in it, and no one at all in the big pool.

Pug and Spencer looked funny, sitting up on their high white platforms, staring down at an empty pool. Of course Pug wore shades, even though it was as dark as evening. And he had his bandanna wrapped around his forehead as always.

Later, I saw him disappear down to the tennis courts with Cassie. He had his arm around her shoulders, and she snuggled against him as they walked.

That was fast! I thought. I guess I was a little jealous.

I mean, I wasn't interested in Pug. But I would've liked to have met a guy that fast.

Seeing Pug and Cassie was the most interesting thing that happened all that day. The club was so quiet and empty.

I think we all felt a little strange. It was like we threw a party and no one showed up.

Everyone was quiet at dinner too. No drama or arm-wrestling competitions like our first night.

Thank goodness!

I didn't realize I was sunburned until I got back to my room after dinner. So stupid of me. I'd borrowed May-Ann's sunblock and carried it around all day, but never put it on.

May-Ann came in as I finished pulling on my nightshirt. She stepped into the room and started grinning.

"What's so funny?" I asked.

"I just keep picturing you last night, coming into this dark room, seeing the little mice figures I had put on the dresser, and thinking they were real!"

We both laughed. It was pretty stupid, I admit. "I really thought they were moving," I told her again. "I was so out of it yesterday."

I walked over to her dresser and admired them again. After May-Ann got Munchy, people started giving her little mice figures. Porcelain mice, stuffed mice, plastic mice. Before she knew it, she had a mouse collection.

Why did she bring her collection with her to the club?

Why did May-Ann do anything? She was truly a weird person.

She walked over to the mirror and started brushing her short auburn hair. She was so tall, she had to bend her knees to see her head in the mirror.

"Going out?" I asked.

She didn't answer. She brushed her hair quickly, then headed out the door. "See you later," she called back.

"Hey, May-Ann—where are you going?" I called.

But she was gone.

That night I woke up drenched in a cold sweat.

My nightshirt clung to my sunburned shoulders. My heart was racing.

I'd been having a nightmare, some kind of scary chase.

The fear lingered, but the dream vanished when I blinked my eyes open.

I squinted through the thick darkness at May-Ann's clock-radio on her bed table. A little after two in the morning.

May-Ann sat up with a start. Her voice came out in a sleep-filled whisper. "Did you hear it too?"

"Huh?" I pulled myself up. My sunburned shoulders ached. I hadn't heard her return.

"Did you hear it?" May-Ann whispered.

I listened hard.

I heard a low moan. From the hall right outside our door.

"There. Hear it?" May-Ann demanded impatiently.

I nodded.

And heard it again.

A low moan. And then a cry, *"Help me. Please— help me."*

Chapter 14

LINDSAY

"Help me—help me."

"Hear it? It's the drowned girl," May-Ann whispered, jumping to her feet.

I hopped up too. A cold chill swept down my back. The bedsheet got tangled around one leg, and I nearly fell.

"Help . . ." A low moan, so faint, so incredibly faint.

"She's out in the hall," May-Ann whispered. "I told you, she haunts the club. You hear it too—don't you?"

I nodded, still groggy from sleep, still feeling the fear of my nightmare. "I hear it too, May-Ann," I whispered. "You're not imagining it."

But I don't believe in ghosts.

That's what I told myself as I followed May-Ann across the bare floor to the door.

"Help me. . . . Please help."

I don't believe in you, I silently told the ghost. So why are you standing outside my bedroom door?

My heart was pounding as we stepped up to the door and pressed our ears against it.

Silence.

Then another low moan. Such a mournful sound. Then a dry whisper, dry as death.

May-Ann gripped the door handle.

I took a step back.

"Hellllp—helllllllp." Right outside. So close. So close.

With a sudden motion, May-Ann turned the knob and yanked the door open.

And we both stared out at the moaning ghost.

Chapter 15

LINDSAY

"**H**elllp me—please."

I goggled, totally stunned.

May-Ann's face registered surprise at first. Then her features knotted in anger. "Cassie!" she shrieked. "You're not funny!"

Cassie started to laugh. She fell against Pug, who grabbed her around the waist, grinning sheepishly at us.

"The—look—the look on your faces!" Cassie managed to choke out through her laughter. Tears ran down her cheeks.

"You're not funny," May-Ann repeated through clenched teeth. She was gripping the doorknob so hard, her hand must have hurt.

"It was Cassie's idea," Pug said, still holding on to her.

Cassie pushed her blond hair away from her face. "You believed it—didn't you?" she accused May-Ann. "You really believed it was a ghost!"

May-Ann didn't reply. She just glared back at Cassie in fury.

My heart finally stopped racing. I started to laugh. I had to admit that Cassie made a pretty convincing ghost. May-Ann was so serious about the club being haunted, she even had me believing it.

It was a relief that it was just Cassie, up to another one of her practical jokes.

"You should be an actress, Cassie," I told her.

She took a short bow. Then she let out another ghostly moan.

Pug and I applauded. I turned to May-Ann, expecting her to lighten up, to join in the joke, or at least admit that Cassie had fooled her.

But to my surprise, May-Ann uttered a loud sob. "You'll be sorry!" she screamed at Cassie with such anger that Cassie and Pug both stopped grinning and stared stonily at May-Ann.

Then May-Ann slammed the door shut, so hard that all the little mice on her dresser jumped.

"May-Ann, it was just a joke," I said, reaching for her shoulder, trying to calm her.

But May-Ann pulled away from me. "Cassie will be sorry," she murmured bitterly. "She'll be sorry. You'll see."

I woke up early the next morning and gazed out the window of our room. The sun was bright red, climbing a clear sky. The air was already hot. The corner of the pool visible from the window sparkled invitingly.

Our first real summer day. I knew the club would be crowded. I showered and dressed, pulling a long-sleeved white T-shirt over my navy blue bathing suit, and hurried to breakfast.

By the time I got to the dining room, Cassie had already told everyone about the joke she had played. Everyone made haunting ghost wails as I entered the room. I laughed. But I knew May-Ann wouldn't find it amusing.

I had to leave before May-Ann came to breakfast. Pug and I had the first shift at the big pool.

I splashed on plenty of sunblock before climbing the platform. The sun was already strong. I kept my T-shirt on. My sunburned shoulders were too tender.

The pool was really crowded by ten-thirty. Three women were doing serious laps in the roped-off lap area. A large group of teenagers, locals who all seemed to be friends, were dunking one another, splashing and acting pretty rowdy down at the deep end.

Gazing across the pool, I had to shield my eyes from the sun even though I was wearing sunglasses. Pug was already surrounded by a group of teenage girls. He was really coming on to them, teasing them, acting like a big shot, really eating up the attention.

He's a good-looking guy, I thought, watching the girls clamor around him. But he isn't *that* good-looking!

I blew my whistle at a boy in huge baggy swim trunks who was trying to shove a smaller boy into the pool. Then my eye caught Cassie, on duty at the kiddie pool just beyond the deep end of the big pool.

Cassie was standing at the edge of the round pool, hands at her waist. She was frowning, staring angrily at Pug.

I guessed she wasn't happy about Pug's female fan club.

My first shift went smoothly. It felt good to be soaking up the sun, watching a noisy, crowded pool. I love the smell of swimming pools, that sweet-tart chlorine smell. I think it's my favorite aroma.

Summer is finally here, I thought happily.

May-Ann appeared a little before eleven. She was giving a lifesaving class every morning in the shallow end. To my surprise, she waved and seemed really cheerful.

I watched her walk to the diving board and dive in. May-Ann was a really graceful diver. Her long legs were straight, and she hardly made a splash.

Arnie replaced me a few minutes after eleven.

I climbed down from the platform, eager to go inside and cool off. A glass of cold water sounded like a good idea.

I had gone only a few steps, the concrete hot under my bare feet, when a voice stopped me. "Look at this. Do you believe this?"

I felt a warm hand on my shoulder. I turned to see Spencer, holding his palm up to my face. "Huh? What's wrong with your hand?" I asked, confused.

"No. Look," he insisted.

I saw a quarter in his palm. "You're showing me a quarter?"

He nodded. His dark eyes sparkled in the sunlight. He adjusted his short ponytail with a toss of his head. "Know what it is?" he asked.

"Yeah. I know what a quarter is," I told him.

"It's a tip," he said, sneering. He lowered his hand. "Some rich woman pressed it into my hand."

I laughed. "She gave you a tip?"

He frowned. "I helped her with her lounge chair. The back was stuck, so I fixed it for her. I started to walk away, and she pushed the quarter into my hand."

"Your lucky day," I said dryly.

"Know what she said to me?" Spencer demanded. "Know what she said?" A grin slowly spread over his face. "She said, 'Put it in your college fund.'"

We both laughed.

"Very generous," I said. "Maybe if you help her with her chair tomorrow, she'll give you another quarter."

His smile faded. He tossed the quarter into a trash basket.

"Hey!" I cried, reaching out—too late—to stop him. "That's money. I think it's against the law to throw it away."

"We're talking big-time crime here," he muttered.

I stared back at him, trying to remember. Trying to remember last summer. Trying to remember something about him.

"Spencer," I started. "Last summer. You and I—"

He glanced at the pool clock. "Uh-oh. I'm late. Got to run. Bye, Lindsay."

"But, Spencer—"

Too late. He was jogging to the deep end of the pool. I stood there, watching him.

I knew Spencer. I definitely knew him. And he knew me.

Then why didn't I remember anything about him?

When he first entered the room on that stormy day, he had seemed so surprised to see me. But then he had seemed glad.

Had there been something between Spencer and me last summer?

Did he and I have a short romance or something?

I had the feeling we did, but I couldn't dredge the memory up. I couldn't dredge up *any* memory about him.

Late that night I awoke and sat up in my narrow bed, drenched in hot sweat, My nightshirt clung to my back. The clock-radio read two forty-five.

Middle of the night.

My head ached. It was so hot, so sticky and hot. I felt as if I were drowning in hot sweat.

I gazed across the dark room. Pale gray light filtered through the window onto May-Ann's bed. May-Ann's empty bed.

Where was she?

I climbed unsteadily to my feet. I made my way to the open window. The air from outside felt as hot as the air inside the room.

I need a swim, I decided, to cool off. A quick dip.

I changed into the swimsuit I had worn that morning. Then, silently, I tiptoed into the hall. I checked both ways. No one in sight.

Of *course* no one is in sight, I scolded myself. It's two o'clock in the morning.

Walking quickly, still bathed in sweat, I made my way out to the pool.

The water glistened under the white floodlights. The blue tiles shimmered. The sky stretched overhead, dotted with thousands of tiny, blinking stars.

The pavement was still warm under my bare feet. The water looked so cool, so inviting.

I stepped to the edge of the shallow end and stared down the length of the pool. Someone had left a white Styrofoam boogie board in the pool. It bobbed near the rope that sectioned off the lap area.

Next to a blue object floating near where the deep water began.

A floating blue object.

A—floating girl!

I gasped as I ran along the side of the pool.

And she came into clear focus.

A girl in a blue bikini. Floating facedown, bobbing with the water. Her blond hair floating on top of the water.

Her skin so white, so unearthly white under the artificial light.

No!

It had to be my imagination. Another hallucination.

I blinked. Then blinked again.

I shut my eyes, trying to force her away.

But when I opened them, she still floated in front of me.

She was real. A real girl, floating, floating so lifelessly.

No!

I plunged into the water. I didn't even take a breath.

I dove in, felt the cold water over me.

I came up sputtering, choking.

Three long strokes. That's all it took to get to the girl.

Three long strokes, and I reached her.

Still coughing, I grabbed her blond hair, tugged it. Tugged her up. Pulled her face out of the water.

So heavy. Her head was so heavy.

I stared at it—stared at her face.

Stared at it and stared at it.

And didn't believe it.

Chapter 16

LINDSAY

Holding her up by the hair, I stared into the dead girl's face.

Stared into *my* face. Lindsay's face.

My own face.

"You—you can't be Lindsay!" I choked out. I held her up, held her up so that her face—my face—was practically touching mine.

"You can't be Lindsay!" I told the dead girl. "Because I am Lindsay!"

Water rolled down her pale forehead.

Her purple, swollen lips opened slowly, and water rolled out and down her chin.

Her eyes, lifeless green eyes, stared back at me blankly.

More water poured out from between the swollen lips.

I heard a choking sound, then the sound of air brushing past the dead lips.

The green eyes rolled up in her head, leaving only white showing.

Another brush of air as more water rolled down her chin.

And then a wet whisper. The purple lips shuddered and moved, and words dribbled out in a wet whisper: *"I'm Lindsay."*

"I'm Lindsay," the dead girl murmured, her solid white eyes glaring at me, so bright under the floodlights.

"No!" I cried. "No!"

And as I held her hair, held up her heavy, water-soaked head, her pale skin began to darken.

Her skin darkened to green. Then it began to droop.

The eyes sank back into the green skin—until I was staring at empty sockets.

Green as seaweed, her skin sagged. It oozed down, down toward the water.

A dull moan escaped the swollen lips.

A clump of skin plopped into the water. Then another.

I still gripped the blond hair, gripped it tightly, held it up as I stared at the disintegrating face.

In seconds the green skin had all slipped off.

And I was left holding a handful of hair, staring in horror at a watery skull.

Chapter 17

LINDSAY

*F*rozen in horror, I gaped into the deep black eye sockets of the skull.

With a choked gasp, I finally let go of the hair.

As the dead girl sank into the water, she began to fade. The water swirled up, splashed against my face, into my eyes.

When I opened my eyes, the girl was gone. . . .

And I was sitting up in bed, drenched in sweat.

The curtains fluttered out from the bedroom window in a soft, warm breeze.

I shuddered and squinted into the gray light.

I pulled the bedsheet up to my chin even though I was hot and sticky. I sat still and waited for the trembling to stop.

It had been a dream, a truly gross dream.

The girl in the pool, the girl with my face—just a nightmare.

Her rotting, wet face lingered in my mind. I shut my eyes, but she didn't go away.

I blinked several times, struggling to force away my nightmare, struggling to focus my eyes in the darkness.

"Lindsay . . ." A whispered voice.

In my dream?

Someone calling to me from my nightmare?

Across the dark room, the curtains snapped noisily, startling me.

"Lindsay . . ." The whispered voice again.

Not in my dream, I realized. I was wide awake now.

I gazed across the room at May-Ann's bed. Still empty.

Where was she?

Where was May-Ann in the middle of the night?

I pushed a lock of damp hair off my forehead. I suddenly thought of my air conditioner at home. The little air conditioner tucked into the window on the left.

I felt a pang of homesickness.

"Lindsay—come here."

The voice was calling me.

Who was it?

Where? Right outside the door.

"May-Ann?" I called out to her for some reason. Was it May-Ann calling to me? Was May-Ann locked out of the room somehow?

No. I hadn't locked the door.

"May-Ann?" I repeated her name—then listened to the silence.

"Lindsay—come out. Lindsay—"

I lowered my feet to the floor. I stood up and yawned.

Who was calling me?

The curtains tossed violently in a sudden gust. I shivered despite the heat.

I pulled a cotton robe over my nightshirt and fumbled in the dark until I managed to slip my feet into a pair of rubber flipflops.

"Lindsay . . ."

A hoarse whisper, just loud enough for me to hear through the door.

"I'm coming!" I called, then yawned again. Still half asleep.

The nightmare lingered in my mind. I saw my dead, water-bloated face again.

I opened the door. No one in the hall.

"Lindsay—come here. . . ." The whisper called me from around the corner.

I stepped into the hall, pulling my robe around me, tying the belt.

I felt so sleepy. Was I really doing this? Was I really out in the hall at three in the morning, following a whispered voice?

I made my way around the corner. I heard a door creak, far down the hall. But I didn't see anyone.

I stopped to listen. Had the whispering stopped? Had the voice disappeared?

"Lindsay—this way."

I began breathing hard. I suddenly realized my hands were cold. What is going *on* here? I wondered.

"May-Ann—is that you?" I asked. My voice came out so soft, I could barely hear it.

"This way . . ." came the whispered reply.

I stopped in front of the dining room doors.

The voice had summoned me—to the dining room.

I pushed the door open. "Who's here?" I managed to choke out.

No reply.

The room was hot, stifling hot.

Orange light flickered against the wall.

It took me a while to realize that a fire was blazing in the fireplace.

A fire at three in the morning?

"Is anybody in here?" I cried, my voice shrill and tight.

I took a few steps into the large room, my eyes on the fire, on the brilliant orange flames.

"Ohh." I uttered a low moan when I saw Cassie.

She was lying facedown in front of the fire, shadows dancing over her.

I saw her sandals first. Then I recognized her baggy green shorts, the shorts she had worn at dinner.

Then I saw the fireplace poker lying beside her on the floor.

"Cassie?" I gasped.

Why was she lying like that? So close to the fire—so close—*too* close!

I let out a wild shriek when I saw the flames leap over her head.

Her head—her head was in the fire.

76

"Cassie? Nooooooo!"

With a loud sob, I grabbed her feet.

I pulled. I pulled with all my might.

The body started to slide.

I pulled harder, pulled her away, pulled her from the leaping, tossing flames.

I was still holding on to both her ankles when I saw that her hair, her face—they were all burned away.

All burned away.

PART TWO

THE OLD GHOST

Chapter 18

DANNY

Why was Lindsay in the dining room at three in the morning?

That question kept repeating in my mind as I watched the police officers do their work.

It wasn't my only question. I also wondered why Cassie had been in the dining room. Why she had built such a big fire. Why someone had murdered her.

Murder.

Had someone broken into the guest house? A burglar, maybe? Had Cassie surprised a burglar and gotten herself killed?

The police hadn't been able to find any sign of a break-in. No broken windows. The doors to the outside were all locked.

"Do you think someone in this room killed Cassie?" I whispered to Pete. He and I were standing by the window, watching the police, alert in case they had more questions for us.

Pete shook his head. His eyes were red and watery. His face was pale, and he looked exhausted. "No. That's impossible," he murmured. But I caught the uncertainty in his eyes.

Two officers continued to examine Cassie's body. Another officer was studying the brass fireplace poker. Another officer, a young woman, was staring thoughtfully into the fireplace.

They had been in the dining room for nearly an hour. The fire had burned down. Purple embers glowed like a dark carpet below the grate.

I glanced over at the other lifeguards. They were huddled around a table, their faces pale, their eyes red-rimmed and tired, their expressions solemn, frightened.

Deirdre had her hands over her face. Her shoulders trembled. I realized she was crying. Pug leaned over her, trying to comfort her.

Spencer's dark hair had fallen over his eyes. He stared down at the table as if in a trance. Arnie had his arms crossed tightly in front of him. His chair was tilted back against the wall. His eyes were closed.

Lindsay and May-Ann sat close together at the far end, away from the others. Their faces were pinched, their mouths set in tight lines.

May-Ann's auburn hair, usually neat and in place, was wild. Lindsay nervously tightened and untightened the belt on her robe. Her chin quivered, but she wasn't crying.

Pete sighed as two grim-faced officers finally covered Cassie's body with a long sheet of black plastic. "Her head—" he muttered to me, swallowing hard. He turned away without finishing his sentence.

The officers had already questioned everyone briefly. Now one of them turned from the fire and made her way to the table, her eyes on Lindsay.

May-Ann scooted over. The woman sat down between Lindsay and May-Ann. "I'm Officer Malone," she said softly. She had large brown eyes in a round face, topped with short black hair. Straight bangs crossed her forehead.

She pulled a small notepad and a ball-point pen from her blue shirt pocket. "Tell me again how you happened to come to the dining room," she asked Lindsay as I moved closer to listen.

Lindsay cleared her throat. Her voice cracked as she started to reply. She cleared her throat once more. "I—I heard a voice. It called me," Lindsay murmured.

Officer Malone narrowed her brown eyes at Lindsay. "A voice?"

Lindsay nodded. Her chin was quivering. She looked really frightened.

"You say you heard a voice? What kind of voice?" Officer Malone asked, scribbling something on her pad. "A man's voice? A woman's? A voice you recognized?"

Lindsay hesitated. "Just a voice," she replied. "It was more of a whisper, actually. I couldn't tell who it was. It just kept whispering my name, telling me to follow it."

Officer Malone frowned. She stared hard at Lindsay, studying her face. "You realize this sounds very strange, don't you?"

Lindsay nodded. She lowered her eyes.

"Are you saying you were sleepwalking?" the woman asked. "Were you dreaming the voice?"

"No," Lindsay replied sharply. "It was real. I heard it. It woke me up. It's true." She let out a short sob. "I know you don't believe me, but—"

"I didn't say that," Officer Malone replied gently. She raised a hand, motioning for Lindsay to calm down. "I just think it's weird. Do you take medication of any kind?"

"Huh?" Lindsay gaped at her. "No."

"Had you been drinking tonight? Beer or anything?"

"No."

"What is your home address?" the officer asked, writing in her pad.

Across the room at the fireplace, I saw an officer down on his knees, poking through the embers with a gloved hand.

Lindsay hesitated. "I live at 212 Fear Street," she answered finally. "It's in Shadyside. About forty miles south of here."

"I know," Officer Malone replied. "Officer Kurtz over there is from Shadyside." She pointed to the man poking through the fire.

"We'll have to talk more about this voice you heard, Lindsay," Officer Malone said. She patted Lindsay on the arm. "But we don't have to talk now. You've been through a horrible shock."

Lindsay nodded her head. Tears finally started to run down her cheeks.

"It's late, but I need to ask a few more questions," Officer Malone said, climbing to her feet to address the others.

Pete and I moved even closer to the table.

Arnie's chair tilted back a little too far. He nearly toppled over backward, but caught himself and managed to regain his balance.

Spencer moved behind Lindsay and placed his hands on her trembling shoulders. He bent down and whispered something to her. I couldn't hear what he said.

I felt a slight pang of jealousy. I realized that I wanted to be the one to comfort Lindsay. I found myself wondering whether Lindsay liked Spencer better than she liked me.

Officer Malone scribbled something in her pad. Then she flipped the page and wrote some more. When she finished writing, she raised her dark eyes to Pug. "You went out with Cassie tonight?"

Pug's cheeks darkened from pink to red. "Yeah. We drove to town after dinner," he replied. He was nervously twirling a class ring on his finger. "We were going to go to a movie. But we ended up just cruising around."

"What time did you get back?" Officer Malone asked.

"Early," Pug told her. He raised his hand. "I don't wear a watch. See? But it was early."

"And when you got back here?" the woman asked.

"We stayed out by the pool a little while," Pug said, twirling the ring. "Then we went to our rooms."

"Did you see Cassie go to her room?" Officer Malone demanded.

Pug nodded. "Yeah. It's right down the hall from mine. I saw her go in."

"I'm her roommate," Deirdre broke in. Her face was puffy and tear stained. "I was in bed, but I heard her come in. It was about eleven-thirty."

"Did you hear Cassie leave the room later?" Officer Malone asked.

Deirdre twisted her face into a thoughtful frown. "No. I didn't," she replied. "I'm a very sound sleeper."

Officer Malone wrote something, then snapped the pad shut. She glanced at her watch. "It's very late," she said. "I'm going to let you all go back to bed while we continue our work."

I glanced out the window and saw two officers examining the pool, leaning over the water, their faces bright from the light shining up from the pool.

"The club will have to be closed tomorrow," Officer Malone told Pete. "Our investigation could take all day. We'll need to have the area untouched."

Pete started to protest, but stopped himself. "I'll have to call the director," he murmured.

"Has anyone called the girl's parents?" Officer Kurtz asked from the fireplace.

The room fell silent.

I glanced down at the plastic covering over the body.

I couldn't believe it was Cassie under there.

The lifeguards started to make their way out. Deirdre was crying. Spencer had an arm around Lindsay's shoulders.

I stayed to help Pete. But he motioned for me to go to my room. "I'll need your help tomorrow," he called.

Out in the hall, May-Ann turned to me. Her dark eyes lit up excitedly. "This happens every summer," she murmured.

"What?" I wasn't sure I'd heard her.

"The police should know," May-Ann said. "Someone dies here every summer."

Up ahead, Lindsay gasped when May-Ann said that.

I stared at May-Ann, startled by her expression.

She had the strangest smile on her face. A gloating smile.

Why is she so happy? I wondered.

Why?

Chapter 19

MOUSE

*H*i, Terry. It's me. Mouse.

I've been dying to call you, Terry. But it's been crazy here.

Police crawling all over the place, poking into every corner.

I guess you know why.

That's right, Terry.

Mouse did it.

I killed one, Terry.

It wasn't that hard. She didn't know what hit her.

I did it for you, Terry. I remember how the lifeguards all laughed at you. I remember the bad-news jokes they pulled.

They pulled them on me too—remember?

Well, now who's getting the bad news? Ha-ha.

That's right.

No one suspects me. Who would suspect innocent-looking Mouse?

No one.

But I've got to pick up the pace. I've got to get another one. And then another one.

I promised you, Terry. And I keep my promises.

I've got to run.

I'll call you after I do the next one, Terry.

I know you can't call me.

Chapter 20

LINDSAY

*T*he day after the police left was sunny and hot. It felt more like August than late June, and the pool was crowded and noisy.

Back to normal, I thought, gazing down from my high perch on the lifeguard platform.

At least, some of us were back to normal.

Pug was on the platform across from me, flirting with a group of giggling girls. One of them, a good-looking girl in a white bikini, stole his whistle— grabbed it right out of his hand and ran off with it.

The other girls laughed. A few minutes later, when his break came, I saw Pug disappearing toward the tennis courts, his arm around another girl, this one in a red bikini.

Back to normal, I sighed.

Wish I could get back to normal.

I concentrated on the swimmers in the pool. A group of kids were having a splashing war in the shallow end. Water splashed up onto my feet.

I blew the whistle. "Cool it, guys!" I called to them. The splashing continued, only less violently.

I congratulated myself. I had gone nearly five minutes without picturing Cassie sprawled on the dining room floor, her head in the fireplace.

Five minutes was a long time.

The day before, the long, dreary day when the club was closed, I had pictured Cassie every time I closed my eyes.

I'd kept to myself most of the day. Spencer asked if I wanted to take a walk or something. But I told him no.

Danny was really considerate too. He kept checking to see if I was okay, if I wanted to talk.

But I didn't want to talk. I didn't want to think either. But I couldn't help it.

I kept picturing Cassie. And I kept hearing the whispered voice, calling me from my room, calling me to the dining room.

I knew that Officer Malone didn't believe me about the voice. I saw the doubt on her face, the way she narrowed her eyes, as if challenging me to change the story.

I didn't blame her.

Who would believe such a weird story?

The only problem was, it was true.

Cassie's murder was so horrifying. It took up so much of my thoughts that I had little time to think about anything else.

I suddenly found myself thinking about my parents.

To my shock, I realized that I hadn't talked to them since I'd arrived at the club.

Almost a week and not a word from them. Why hadn't they called to make sure I had arrived?

And why hadn't I thought of calling them?

This is definitely weird, I thought. The Becks are a family that believes in constant communication.

On my break I hurried to my room. It would feel so good to talk to them, to tell them about the horrible murder, to assure them I was okay.

And maybe they could clear up a few mysteries for me. Maybe they could clear up the mystery of why I had arrived with a two-year-old ID card. And maybe they could tell me something about Spencer Brown. I might have talked to them about Spencer after I went home last summer.

Eagerly I burst into my room, dropped onto the edge of my bed, and reached for the phone. I listened for a dial tone, then punched in my home number.

It rang twice.

Then a pause.

Then I heard a recorded woman's voice say: *"We're sorry, but the number you have called is no longer in service."*

Chapter 21

LINDSAY

I realized I must have dialed wrong. So I hung up and then punched the number in again, carefully pushing each number.

Two rings. Three. Then the same taped message: *"We're sorry, but the number you have called is no longer in service."*

I listened to the tape repeat three times before I hung up. Then I slumped over on the edge of the bed, just staring at the phone, trying to figure out what I was doing wrong.

My parents' number *had* to be in service. No way their phone would be turned off. No way.

I had a sick feeling in the pit of my stomach.

What was wrong?

"Hey!" I cried out as a thought struck me.

The storm. A brief thunderstorm had roared

through yesterday afternoon. It lasted only an hour. But it could have messed up the phone lines. That happened a lot. And that explained why I couldn't get through to my parents.

Feeling a little better, I picked up the phone again and called the operator. "I'm having trouble getting through to my house," I told her. "Could you dial it for me?"

"What is the number, please?" Her voice sounded tinny and far away. There was a lot of static on the line.

I told her the number. I could hear clicks as she dialed it for me.

It rang twice. Then the same taped message came on.

I could feel the panic tightening my throat. This was *so weird*.

Was I calling the wrong number? Had I forgotten my own phone number?

I hung up and dialed long distance information. My throat suddenly felt dry. My hand was shaking a little.

"Information for what city?" asked a male operator.

"For Shadyside," I told him. "Could you tell me the number of Mr. and Mrs. Austin Beck on Fear Street?"

There was a long pause.

Please find it. Please find it! I silently urged.

It shouldn't be this hard to call home, I told myself, gripped with cold fear. I've never had any problem before.

What is happening here? *What?*

Suddenly the operator's voice came back on the line. "Could you spell that name, please?"

"B-e-c-k," I said, practically shouting the letters. "Beck. On Fear Street."

He disappeared again. Another long silence.

I pressed the receiver hard against my ear, listening to the low, crackling sound.

Finally he came back on once again. "I'm sorry, miss," he said. "There's no listing in Shadyside for anyone named Beck."

Chapter 22

LINDSAY

I sat and stared at the phone until it became a white blur. My heart was racing. I could feel the blood pulsing at my temples.

Why couldn't I reach my parents?

Why did the operator say they weren't listed?

They *had* to be listed. They *had* to be there! I had seen them less than a week ago.

What is going on? I wondered. Why haven't they called?

Has something terrible happened?

I had to find out—right away.

Taking a deep breath to slow the pounding of my heart, I got to my feet and hurried outside.

I spotted Danny across the pool, talking with May-Ann. Her lifesaving class had just ended. Her students were still practicing head holds in the shallow end of the pool.

Danny held up his clipboard. May-Ann leaned close to him to read what he was showing her.

"Danny—can I borrow your car?" I cried breathlessly, jogging up to them. The pavement was burning my bare feet. I stepped into Danny's shadow, hoping the shade would be cooler.

May-Ann's green swimsuit was soaked. Her auburn hair clung wetly to her head. She gazed up from the clipboard and frowned. "I hoped you could take my afternoon shift," she said. She rubbed her shoulder. "I think I just pulled a muscle or something during class."

"I—I can't!" I cried. I hadn't meant to sound so shrill, so out of control. But I couldn't help it. "I have to go home. I really do!"

May-Ann pulled off her sunglasses and squinted at me. I could see she was startled by how frantic I sounded.

Danny lowered his clipboard. "Did you hear something from home? Bad news?"

I shook my head. "No. But I have to drive home. I have to see my parents."

Danny frowned. His eyes ran down the clipboard. "Did you call them?"

"I can't!" I cried shrilly. "I can't reach them! Something—something is wrong!"

May-Ann rubbed her shoulder. "Ow," she groaned. "What did I *do*?"

"Can I borrow the car?" I pleaded. "Shadyside is less than an hour from here, Danny."

Danny stared at the clipboard fretfully. "Can you be back to relieve Arnie for the last afternoon shift?" he asked.

"Yeah. Sure," I answered quickly. "I'll hurry right back. Promise."

"Ow." May-Ann let out another groan. "I hope I only twisted it. I've got another lifesaving class at three."

"I'll get you the keys," Danny said, starting toward the guest house. "Follow me."

I hurried after him. He turned and called back to May-Ann. "Try swimming it off. The water might help."

"Thanks, Doc!" she called back.

"See you later!" I called. Then I followed Danny to the guest house to get the car keys.

I feel better already, I thought.

Mom will sure be surprised to see me.

It took nearly an hour to drive to Shadyside.

About half an hour from the club, a little blue convertible had collided with an enormous grain truck. The front end of the car was completely crushed. The truck was turned sideways. And there was yellow grain—piles of it—all over the highway.

Only one lane remained open. Drivers slowed to gawk at the wrecked car and all the grain.

I sat sweltering in Danny's little green Corolla. The car didn't have an air conditioner. I had all the windows down, but the breeze was hot and dusty.

Let's go, let's go, let's go! I silently chanted, drumming my fingers impatiently on the wheel.

I don't think I had ever been so eager to get home.

I knew my mom would be able to clear up all the mysteries.

Why hadn't she and Dad called when they didn't hear from me?

Why couldn't I reach them? Why did I keep getting that same taped message: "We're sorry, but the number you have called is no longer in service."

Why was my North Beach Country Club ID card two years old? Why did I keep seeing that girl drowning, a girl in a blue bikini?

Why? Why? Why? The questions hounded me all the way to Shadyside.

As I finally turned onto Fear Street, my heart was pounding.

I rolled past the familiar houses, covered in the shade of bent, old trees. Trees formed an arch over the street, their thick leaves nearly blocking out all the light.

Only the burned-out Simon Fear mansion stood bathed in sunlight, as if under a bright spotlight, up on the low, sloping hill that overlooked the cemetery.

A few moments later my block came into view. The Millers' house with their hideous, grinning lawn gnome in the center of a petunia bed. The flat, empty lot covered with tall grass, where my friends and I played soccer and softball. The Hogans' sprawling wreck of a house with its shingles still in need of a paint job.

Finally my house came into view. I slowed the car as I neared it. The house was a two-story square, faded white clapboard with dark green shutters framing the windows.

"Mom, I'm here," I murmured out loud, my heart racing.

I knew Dad would be at work. But Mom had to be home. She *had* to be!

No car in sight. I turned sharply and inched the car up the driveway.

The front door was open. I could see only darkness behind the screen door.

I shifted into park and cut the engine. I stared eagerly out through the passenger window.

Hey, where's the apple tree? I wondered.

The apple tree that had stood next to the driveway had been cut down. Not even a stump remained. Dad had been threatening to cut it down for years because it dropped its apples all over the drive.

I climbed out of the car and slammed the door.

I stretched. I was wearing a green polo shirt over white tennis shorts. The shirt clung to my back.

They put in a new flower bed, I saw, just past the front stoop. Red and white impatiens. Very pretty.

From the front walk, I saw movement in the window.

She's home! I told myself happily.

I ran up the walk, leapt up the two steps onto the front stoop, and eagerly pulled open the screen door.

"Mom!" I cried.

Chapter 23

LINDSAY

*T*he woman dropped the vase of flowers she was holding.

The glass shattered loudly. The flowers tumbled to her feet and lay in a spreading puddle of water.

Her pale blue eyes fixed stonily on me. "Who—who *are* you?" she cried.

She had short black hair streaked with gray. She was small and frail-looking. Her shoulders were hunched up inside a flowered housedress that appeared too large for her.

I had never seen her before.

I guessed that she was a new neighbor.

"I'm so sorry I frightened you," I managed to choke out, staring down at the flowers scattered over the floor. "Is—is my mom home?"

"Your mom?"

The woman stepped back, away from the puddle of water. One long flower clung to the top of her shoe.

"Is she home?" I repeated, my throat suddenly dry.

"I'm the only one home," the woman replied, kicking the flower off her shoe. "Are you in the wrong house?"

"No," I answered quickly. "I live here, but—"

My eyes wandered around the small living room. The green chairs, the matching couch. Strange new flower paintings on the wall.

Had my parents redecorated?

"You can't just barge in here," the woman said, the color returning to her cheeks. She placed her hands on her waist. Her eyes narrowed, inspecting me warily.

"But this is my house," I insisted. "Do you know when my mom will be back? Is she—?"

The woman stared at me in silence. I could see fear in her pale blue eyes.

Did she think I had come to rob her?

What was she doing in my house?

"You'd better leave," she said coldly.

"You don't understand," I replied, my voice high and shrill. "I live here. I'm looking for—"

"Whom are you looking for?" the woman asked sharply. "Who are you?"

"I'm Lindsay," I told her. "Lindsay Beck. You see—"

She let out a sharp gasp. "The Becks' daughter?" Her hands shot up to her cheeks.

"Yes," I replied.

"You're looking for the Becks' daughter?" the woman asked. Her face went white and her pale eyes watered over.

"No," I started.

But she interrupted. "The Becks' daughter? Didn't you hear?"

"Hear what?" I asked, feeling my throat tighten.

"I'm so sorry to tell you," the woman said, her hands still pressed against her face. "But she died."

"Huh?" I choked out a startled cry.

"The Becks' daughter—she died," the woman said, her watery eyes locked on mine. "She died two years ago." She slowly lowered her hands. Her frail shoulders slumped forward. "Such a tragedy," she murmured. "Such a terrible tragedy."

"But that's *impossible!*" I shrieked in a terrified voice I didn't recognize.

The woman shut her eyes. She shuddered. "When I bought this house, the Becks were still shattered. Shattered. They wanted to move away from here as fast as they could. Move away and never come back. They—they just went to pieces."

"No!" I screamed. "No! You're wrong! You're wrong!"

The woman opened her eyes. I could see the fear return. My outburst was frightening her.

"I'm so sorry," she said, taking another step back into the room. *My* living room. Mine! With all the unfamiliar furniture and unfamiliar paintings.

My living room. My house.

"But I'm Lindsay Beck!" I screamed. "I'm Lindsay!"

She didn't say anything. She pressed her lips tightly

together and stared back at me with those pale, watery eyes.

"So sorry," she murmured. "I'm so sorry I had to be the one to tell you."

"No!" I screamed. "No!"

Then, without even realizing what I was doing, I whirled around. I ran. Ran through the dark entryway.

I heard the screen door slam behind me as I leapt off the stoop and ran to the driveway.

Dived into the car and sped away.

"I'm Lindsay Beck!" I screamed as I drove. "I'm Lindsay Beck! I'm Lindsay!"

Why did she say I was dead?

Chapter 24

LINDSAY

I must have driven around for hours.

It was dark when I got back to the club.

I didn't remember where I had been all afternoon and evening. Just driving around in circles? Driving around my old neighborhood? Had I parked somewhere? Had I eaten lunch?

I couldn't remember anything that happened after I left my house.

As I pulled Danny's car into the employee lot, I could see the empty pool shimmering darkly under the tall floodlights. It was a sultry night. Nothing moved. Not a leaf on a tree.

It was all as still as a painting. As still as death.

I climbed out, slammed the door, made my way toward the guest house as if in a daze.

Had I left the car keys in the ignition? Had I turned off the headlights?

I didn't remember.

"I don't want to see anyone," I said out loud.

They were probably all in the dining room, finishing dinner. I couldn't face them now. I couldn't face their staring eyes, their questions.

"Lindsay—where were you?"

"Lindsay—why did you miss your shift?"

"Lindsay—why did you go home so suddenly?"

"Lindsay—why do you look so upset?"

"Lindsay? Lindsay? Lindsay?"

I entered through the side door and hurried down the carpeted corridor—past the dining room. I could hear their laughing voices on the other side of the door. Past the common room. Then a sharp turn, and down the narrow, empty hallway.

I was heading to Pete's office.

I had to find my file. I had to read what it said about me.

I'll find my phone number, I told myself, my sneakers thudding loudly over the carpet, my footsteps echoing in the long, empty corridor.

I'll find my phone number. My address. I'll call my parents.

Everything will be in my file. Everything.

It will all be straightened out. All the mysteries.

There's *got* to be a sensible explanation.

I kept picturing the frail little woman standing in my living room with the wet flower stuck to the top of her shoe. Staring at me with those pale, watery eyes. Telling me that I was dead.

That I died two years ago.

"What a terrible tragedy."

But there *had* to be a sensible explanation.

The answer would be in my file.

If the door is locked, I'll break it down! I told myself.

Pete's office was at the end of the west wing of the main lodge. I stopped outside the door. I brushed my damp hair back off my forehead.

I took a deep breath. I reached for the doorknob.

It turned easily. I pushed the door in and entered the dark office.

I fumbled against the wall till I found the light switch. As the light came on, I saw Pete's small, green metal desk. It had a single file folder on it, a small glass clock, a speakerphone, a clipboard, and his metal whistle.

Against the wall, I saw three tall file cabinets.

How will I ever find the right drawer? The right file? I wondered, hesitating by the door.

I stepped inside and carefully closed the door behind me.

If anyone came by and found me in here, it would be really hard to explain. But I didn't care. I had to have some answers—and right away.

I made my way to the file cabinet on the left and squinted at the label on each drawer. The label on the top drawer read FINANCIAL. The second drawer was marked MEMBERSHIPS.

I squatted down to read the label on the third file drawer: EMPLOYMENT.

"Yes!" I whispered.

I pulled open the drawer. It was jammed with files.

I got down on my knees and examined them. The files had employee names at the top, in alphabetical order.

"That wasn't so hard," I murmured out loud.

I began pushing through the front of the files. "Alcorn—Amos—Anders—Ball—Beck."

Beck, Lindsay.

My hand started to shake. It took me three tries to pull the file out of the jammed drawer.

"Here I am, here I am," I whispered to myself.

Holding the file tightly, I climbed to my feet and carried it over to the desk.

"Lindsay Beck." I read the name on it again, just to make sure.

I hesitated.

I suddenly felt hot all over. Hot and cold. My skin prickled. My mouth felt dry.

My hands were shaking.

I struggled to get the file folder open.

Finally I managed it. I pulled out the papers, set them down on the desk, and leaned over them to read them.

I skimmed quickly over familiar statistics. My birth date. My place of birth. My parents' names.

My eyes landed at the bottom of the first page.

I read the words over and over.

"No—I don't believe it!" I shrieked. "I don't believe it!"

Chapter 25

LINDSAY

*T*here's *got* to be a mistake! I told myself.

I gripped the edge of the desk with both hands. I knew that if I let go, I'd fall.

Fall and keep falling. And never get up.

I stared down at the word scribbled in dark blue in large letters across the bottom of the page: DECEASED.

"But that's impossible!" I cried out loud. "I'm alive! I'm not dead!"

I lifted off the top sheet of paper and tossed it aside. A newspaper headline was taped to the second page.

I gaped at the faded headline, swallowing hard.

SHADYSIDE GIRL, 15, DROWNS
IN CLUB POOL

My eyes blurred over. I struggled to read the article, but I couldn't.

I couldn't see. I couldn't think.

I raised the clipping to my face and squinted hard at it.

A tragic accident at the North Beach Country Club . . . Lindsay Beck, 15, drowned. . . . Attempts to resuscitate her failed. . . . Her first year as lifeguard at the club . . . Off duty at the time . . .

I struggled to make sense of the words.

My eyes rose to the date at the top of the clipping. It was two years old.

Two years ago.

The story said that I had drowned two years ago.

It didn't make sense. No sense at all.

And then it hit me all at once.

I dropped to my knees, stunned and shaken.

I dropped to my knees and hugged myself, hugged myself tighter and tighter.

It hit me. It hit me. It suddenly came so horrifyingly clear to me:

I am the dead lifeguard.

PART THREE

TWO GHOSTS

Chapter 26

MOUSE

*H*i, Terry. It's me—Mouse.

How's it going?

Yeah. I know. I haven't called for a while. But don't worry. I've been thinking about you.

You're always on my mind, Terry.

I've been real busy being a lifeguard, see. I wish you could see me, Terry. I really do.

I'm getting a good tan, best I ever had. I'm looking good, Terry. Looking real good.

It's not like before, Terry. Not when you and I were together here.

Being a lifeguard and sitting up on the high white platform where everyone can see you—it's real different.

I wish you weren't dead, Terry. You would've made a great lifeguard. Really. I know that you would.

This would've been our summer. Why'd you have to go and die?

Now you can't answer me back when I call you.

I know you're there. And I know what you want me to do.

You want me to do something terrible—don't you, Terry? You want me to kill another lifeguard.

Well, I haven't forgotten.

I have someone picked out. I'm ready. Really. Mouse is all ready.

Ready to rock 'n' roll, huh?

I know. I know what you're thinking. I'm cold. Real cold.

Well, dead is about as cold as you can get, right?

You want me to kill them all, don't you, Terry?

No problem.

Chapter 27

LINDSAY

"Hey, Arnie—get off the phone and join the party!" Danny called.

Across the dining room, Arnie mumbled a few more words into the phone, then replaced the receiver. "Can I help it if I'm popular?" he called, returning to the table.

"How many times a day do you call your mom?" Deirdre joked.

Everyone laughed.

Arnie's slender face turned bright red. "It wasn't my mom," he muttered, dropping into his seat and grabbing his hamburger.

"I know who Arnie was calling," Pug broke in, grinning. "It was his personal trainer. Arnie was asking for his money back!"

Everyone laughed again.

Arnie stared down at his plate and pretended we didn't exist.

"I think we should get off Arnie's case," Danny suggested. "Give him a break. Why do we always have to pick on Arnie?"

"Because he's Arnie!" Pug declared.

Arnie dropped the hamburger onto his plate and glared at Pug. "I'll take you on in the weight room, dude."

Pug's grin grew wider. "Huh? Say what?"

"A weight-lifting competition," Arnie replied, his cheeks still bright red. One hand tapped the edge of his plate nervously. "Come on, big talker. How about it? You and me. One on one."

Pug jumped to his feet. He grinned down at Arnie. "You're serious?" he cried. "You're *serious?*"

"Whoa—down, boy!" Danny called from the end of the long table. I could see Danny was getting a little upset.

I was sitting next to Arnie, and I had to dodge out of the way as Pug made a leap for him, his hands outstretched. "Here's the weight-lifting competition!" Pug cried.

He grabbed Arnie and lifted him out of his chair.

"Whoa—hey—guys!" Danny jumped to his feet too. "Hey—how about a civilized dinner?"

Pug let out a loud *whoop*. And swung Arnie over his shoulder. I don't think he heard Danny yelling for him to quit.

"Let go, you jerk!" Arnie screamed.

But Pug lifted Arnie with both hands, pushed him

up above his head, lowered him, pushed him up again—as if he were lifting weights.

Arnie thrashed and squirmed and tried to get free.

We were all laughing our heads off. I mean, it was pretty funny.

"That's what I call a good workout!" Pug declared, lowering Arnie to the floor.

Arnie spun around and swung a fist at Pug's head. Pug ducked easily out of the way.

Danny moved quickly to step between them and break it up. He made them shake hands.

"Just goofing," Pug told Arnie.

Arnie scowled. "You're a real riot," he muttered bitterly.

Things calmed down after that. Spencer did a really good impression of a rich woman who comes to the club every afternoon, carrying a tiny baby in one hand, smoking a cigarette with the other.

Spencer is really merciless when it comes to the rich members of the club. He does the cruelest imitations of them. He always cracks everyone up.

Watching him strut back and forth, pretending to drop his cigarette down the baby's shirt, I laughed out loud.

It was two days after my trip home to Shadyside. I hadn't laughed much since returning to the club. I had spent a lot of time thinking hard about myself, about last summer and the summer before, trying desperately to remember.

But I couldn't remember much.

I knew I wasn't dead.

I knew the file in Pete's office had to be wrong

somehow. And the woman living in my old house on Fear Street—she had to be wrong too.

It was all some kind of weird mistake.

I was alive.

I wasn't one of May-Ann's ghosts.

But what was the explanation?

I had spent hours on the phone, trying to locate my parents. But no luck.

Danny had been very understanding. He didn't get on my case for coming back so late to the club. And he gave me a lot of space, to think and to try to keep myself together.

He was a really great guy.

May-Ann had been nice too. She said she knew I was going through a hard time. She said if I needed anyone to talk to, I could always talk to her. Which was great of her.

But sometimes when we were in the room together, I would catch her staring at me. Focusing on me as if I were some kind of lab specimen, or as if I were Munchy and should be in a cage too.

May-Ann probably thinks I'm crazy, I realized.

As troubled as I was, I tried to push all my puzzling, frightening thoughts away and just have a good time.

This was the first night—the first night since Cassie's murder—that everyone seemed to be almost normal.

Spencer was on his feet, impersonating an old man wading in the kiddie pool. Spencer's imitations were hilarious!

Arnie leaned over to whisper something to me. I nodded. I couldn't really hear him.

When I looked up, May-Ann was saying something about the ghosts of the drowned and how the club is cursed.

"May-Ann, give it a rest!" Pug called irritably from across the table.

"You don't believe me," May-Ann continued. "But—"

"Just shut up!" Pug screamed. "We're all sick of hearing about your drowned kids and stupid ghosts! We've had a *real* murder here—remember?"

"Yeah!" Deirdre agreed loudly. "Let's try to forget all the gloomy stuff and not spoil the whole summer!"

May-Ann's cheeks turned pink, and her dark eyes flashed angrily. She clasped her hands tightly together under the table.

"What's your problem anyway?" Pug demanded. "Why can't you lighten up?"

I felt bad for May-Ann. She didn't deserve to be attacked like that.

"Give her a break," I told Pug and Deirdre. "I think May-Ann's stories are interesting."

"You would!" Pug shot back. "You mope around here as if *you're* a ghost!"

"Hey, guys, wait—" Danny tried to break in. He raised both hands in a gesture for everyone to stop.

But it didn't work. Everyone started shouting at once.

I felt a warm hand on my wrist. Arnie leaned close. "Let's get out of here," he whispered in my ear. "Get some fresh air—okay?"

I nodded. "Yeah. Sure." *Anything* to get out of there!

119

Arnie and I jumped up and hurried out of the dining room. The loud, angry voices followed us out into the hall.

Arnie shook his head. "One big happy family," he muttered. He grinned at me. "If I wanted to hear fighting at dinner, I could've stayed home!"

We headed out to the pool area. The pool water splashed softly, a soothing sound.

I took a deep breath and gazed up at the evening sky. We had been at dinner longer than usual. The sun had just gone down, leaving trails of purple and pink through the wisps of low-hanging cloud. A pale half-moon was still low on the horizon.

We made our way past the pool, heading along the walk that led to the tennis courts.

Arnie had his hands stuffed into the pockets of his baggy shorts. He wore a tight blue muscle shirt and walked with his chest puffed out.

"How are you doing?" I asked him, an awkward try at starting a conversation. "It's been so grim here. Do you think we can save the rest of the summer?"

He chuckled to himself, as if I had said something funny. "Summer hasn't really started yet," he replied.

"What's that supposed to mean?" I asked, trying to sound light and casual.

He shrugged. "I've got big plans for this summer," he said.

We passed the tennis courts. The path suddenly grew dark. We were in a small, secluded wooded area that separated the golf course from the rest of the club.

"I had big plans too," I confessed. "I'd been looking forward to this summer for a long time. But—*hey!*"

Without warning, Arnie grabbed me by both shoulders.

His tiny eyes lit up and a strange smile crossed his lips.

He shoved me back—hard—against a wide tree trunk.

"Big plans," he whispered. "Big plans."

I raised both hands and struggled to push him away.

"Arnie—let go!" I cried. "Arnie—what are you *doing?*"

Chapter 28

SPENCER

I couldn't stay in that dining room another second.

Pug, Deirdre, and May-Ann were all going at it, having a great time, yelling and wailing, accusing one another of this and that, ripping one another apart.

Pug seemed to be enjoying the arguing. Pug loves to be the center of attention. That's for sure.

Danny was really upset. I think it was because no one was listening to him—the big cheese—when he told them to sit down and shut up.

Anyway, with all the shouting and carrying on, I really felt as if my head were about to explode.

Why am I sitting here, listening to this? I asked myself.

Lindsay and Arnie had already left a few minutes before. So I ducked out too.

I didn't know where I was going. I just had to get some fresh air.

I trotted outside and did some stretching exercises in front of the pool. Then I started jogging toward the woods.

It was a hot, wet night, and I worked up a sweat right away. It felt good to be moving. I gazed up at the evening sky, streaked with scarlet and purple.

It was so quiet and peaceful when the club closed at night. The only sound was the soft thud of my hightops on the pavement as I jogged.

There was some talk of adding rooms so that guests could stay at the club. I would hate that. Having to be on duty twenty-four hours a day. I liked seeing people arrive in the morning and leave at dinnertime.

I liked having the evenings to myself.

If only the others would forget about Cassie and get back into party moods, I thought. If only everyone could settle down and stop fighting.

I could hear Pug's voice all the way from the dining room.

Pug. The perfect lifeguard. He has a lifeguard body and a lifeguard brain, I told myself.

Was I jealous?

Yeah. A little.

I had just passed the tennis courts and was starting into a small, dark patch of trees, when I heard a shrill scream.

I recognized Lindsay's voice at once.

I stopped jogging, leaned forward to listen, breathing hard.

"Arnie—stop!" she was crying.

I straightened up and began to run. I spotted them in the shadows a few seconds later.

Arnie had Lindsay's back pressed against a tree. He was holding her arms down against her sides.

Lindsay was struggling.

I think Arnie was trying to kiss her.

"Hey!" I shouted, running hard.

Arnie backed off instantly.

He was apologizing as I ran up beside them. "What's going on?" I asked breathlessly.

I was prepared to push Arnie away. But he was already backing up, telling Lindsay how sorry he was, how he didn't mean anything.

Arnie scurried away like a guilty dog with his tail between his legs.

Lindsay rubbed her arms. "He—hurt me," she murmured.

"Are you okay?" I asked.

She nodded.

"What's his problem?" I demanded, turning in the direction Arnie had run. He had vanished from view.

Lindsay shrugged. "He just grabbed me. I—I was so surprised," she stammered.

"Arnie's a little creep," I said.

Lindsay frowned. "Lots of times at the pool I glance over and catch him watching me."

"I watch you too sometimes," I confessed.

We started walking side by side, through the woods toward the golf course. I said something about how quiet it was out there away from Pug and Deirdre and May-Ann. But she didn't seem to hear me.

After we'd made it through the woods, she suddenly stopped and grabbed my arm. "Spencer," she said softly. She had a very thoughtful, solemn expression on her face.

I brushed a leaf from her hair. She had such soft, fine blond hair.

"Spencer, can I ask you a question? About last summer?" she asked hesitantly. Her hand was still on my arm.

"Yeah. Sure," I told her.

It had grown very dark. Back in the trees, crickets began to chirp.

"Well—" Lindsay started to say. "Last summer. Were you and I— I mean—were we good friends?"

I stared at her. Even in the darkness, I could see how stressed out she was.

"Well, Lindsay," I said softly, "you left so suddenly, we didn't have much time to get to know each other."

My answer startled her. Her mouth formed a small *O* of surprise. Her eyes burned into mine.

"I left suddenly?" she asked.

I nodded.

"Why?" she demanded, squeezing my arm. "Why did I leave suddenly, Spencer?"

I just stared at her. I didn't know what to say.

I mean, didn't she *remember?*

Didn't she *know?*

I knew one thing for certain: if she *didn't* remember, I sure wasn't going to be the one to tell her!

Chapter 29

LINDSAY

The next afternoon, another hot, sultry day, I was on duty at the deep end of the pool. Gazing toward the shallow end, I saw Arnie hang up the pay phone. He waved to me and started toward me.

Oh, no, I groaned to myself.

I had avoided Arnie all day. I couldn't stop thinking about that frightening moment in the woods.

He looked even scrawnier than usual in a pair of baggy orange swim trunks that came down nearly to his knees. His bare chest was hairless and bright pink from a fresh sunburn. The sunlight caught the silver ring in his ear.

He stopped beside my platform and gazed up at me without smiling.

"Arnie, what do you want?" I asked sharply.

"To apologize," he answered softly, avoiding my hard stare.

I didn't say anything.

"Lindsay, I'm really sorry about last night," Arnie said. The words came out in a steady monotone. It sounded as if he had rehearsed them.

"I'm sorry too," I said coldly.

"I really acted like a creep," Arnie continued, frowning. "I—I didn't mean to act so rough. Really. I started to kiss you and—and I didn't realize . . ." His voice broke.

I stared hard at him, trying to decide if he was being sincere. I decided maybe he was.

"Apology accepted," I said curtly. I turned my eyes to the pool. Three kids were having a floating race. Another kid was trying to hit them with a beach ball.

"No. Really," Arnie said as if he didn't believe me. "I'm not a bad guy, Lindsay. I'm not like that. I just—I just messed up, that's all."

"It's okay, Arnie," I told him. "Thanks for apologizing. I think I overreacted too, last night."

He rubbed his short brown hair. "Want to go to town tonight?" he asked. "Go to a movie or something? There's a new Bruce Willis film—"

I cut him off. "Not tonight," I said, keeping my eyes on the pool.

He nodded. "But some other night?" he asked, leaning on the side of the platform.

"Maybe," I replied.

"How about Friday night?" Arnie asked.

Luckily, I didn't have to answer. Pete was shouting for Arnie to get over to the kiddie pool—and Arnie hurried away.

Even though Arnie had apologized, I realized I was still a little afraid of him.

He's so eager, I thought, watching him jog through a group of kids.

Too eager. Too desperate.

Frightening . . .

When I turned back toward the pool, I was startled to find a woman staring at me.

She was a middle-aged woman, short and plump, with frizzy black hair over a round, plain face. She wore a bright yellow shirt tied at the waist over a black swimsuit and carried a large, bright yellow beach bag.

"You—" she murmured. She stared at me wide-eyed, in total shock.

I stared back. Did I know this woman?

No . . .

"I remember you," she said, her cheeks turning red. And then she stared even harder at me, narrowing her eyes. "Are you—okay?" she stammered.

I felt so confused. What did she *mean?*

"Yeah—I'm okay," I replied.

"But—" The woman started to say something, then stopped herself. She stared at me a bit longer, raising a hand to her chin.

She shook her head. "Sorry," she murmured. "I thought . . ." Her voice trailed off. She hurried away.

What is her *problem?* I asked myself.

Why did she look so shocked to see me? So shocked she could barely speak?

"I'm alive!" I wanted to shout after her. *"I'm Lindsay Beck, and I'm alive!"*

So why did she stare at me as if she were seeing a ghost?

Chapter 30

LINDSAY

Dinner was pretty tense.

Everyone tried to pretend that the fighting and arguing of the night before hadn't taken place. Spencer did an imitation of a woman trying to coax her three kids out of the pool. Pug told a story about his high school football team getting completely lost in another city on a trip to an away game.

Everyone tried to laugh and talk. But even without any arguing, things were tense.

There was a ghost at the table. Cassie's ghost. She haunted us even though we couldn't see or hear her.

I'd been thinking a lot about ghosts, naturally.

That made *two* ghosts at the club, I thought bitterly, forcing myself to eat the hot dog on my plate.

Two ghosts—Cassie and me.

I gazed at May-Ann. I wondered what she'd say if I

told her I was the dead lifeguard. If I told her about the newspaper clipping that said I had drowned.

I hadn't told anyone. I couldn't.

Not till I knew the explanation.

Not till I knew why the paper had written those lies about me.

After dinner I wandered out by the pool for a while. It was a hazy, hot evening. The sky was still a pale blue, although patchy clouds were floating in from the distance. A red ball of a sun was starting to lower itself behind the trees that hid the golf course.

I sat down by the pool and tried to read. I had a mystery novel that was supposed to be good. But I couldn't concentrate. I was in no mood for any more mysteries!

I felt restless, uncomfortable. The lounge chair stuck to the back of my tank top.

I decided to take a walk. Maybe go to the golf course and back.

I wandered past the guest house and was approaching the small building that housed the exercise room, when I heard voices. Angry voices.

I stopped and peered over the hedge that bordered the path. The lowering sun beamed down onto the ground in front of the building, making everything rosy and unreal.

Staring into the patch of red sunlight, I saw Pug and May-Ann. They were standing in front of the door to the weight room.

May-Ann had an oversize yellow T-shirt pulled down over green spandex bike shorts. She had a tennis racket slung over her shoulder.

Pug wore a blue muscle shirt and faded denim cutoffs. He was gesturing wildly with both hands, shaking his head as he talked.

May-Ann shouted at him at the same time.

I leaned forward against the hedge, curious to hear what they were arguing about.

"Just keep your big mouth shut!" I heard May-Ann shout angrily.

"Maybe I will, maybe I won't!" Pug shot back.

They started shouting together again. But a low-flying jet cut overhead, its roar drowning out their words.

What could Pug and May-Ann possibly be fighting about? I wondered, bewildered.

I had never seen them say two words to each other. They didn't seem at all interested in each other.

So what could they be fighting about?

Suddenly, as I watched them argue, a shadow rolled over me, over the hedge in front of me.

With a shudder, I realized I was no longer alone.

Chapter 31

LINDSAY

I turned to see that Deirdre had slipped up beside me. She had a blue and red Cubs cap pulled down over her short black hair.

"Do you believe that pig?" she said in a low voice. She pointed over the hedge toward Pug.

I opened my mouth to answer, but Deirdre didn't give me a chance. "He's had his pick of every girl at this club," she said, practically spitting out the words. "And now he's hitting on May-Ann." She shook her head in disgust.

The sun lowered behind the trees. Long shadows slid along the ground.

"I could kill him. I really could," Deirdre murmured.

"Not *really*," I said, thinking of Cassie.

Deirdre frowned. "No. Of course not. Not really.

133

Sorry, Lindsay. I guess that was a bad choice of words. I didn't mean *really* kill him."

She sighed. "But I can't believe he's going after May-Ann now."

"They're fighting," I told her. "I don't really think Pug is May-Ann's type."

"Oh, yeah?" Deirdre asked, challenging me. "Then why are they going off together so cozily?"

I turned back to the exercise building in time to see May-Ann and Pug disappear inside, arm in arm.

"Weird," I muttered. "Totally weird."

"Tell me about it," Deirdre replied bitterly.

Later, back in the room, I tried calling my parents one more time. I almost burst into tears when I got the same recorded message.

I had called so many times. And I had tried information again and again, with no success.

I sat on the edge of the bed, staring at the phone, wishing it would ring, *willing* it to ring. I could hear Munchy rattling around in his cage, but I didn't go over to check on him.

"Hey!" I cried out as an idea flashed into my mind. Why hadn't I thought of it sooner?

I dialed information and got the phone number of my only other relative, my aunt Billie in Burlington. Eagerly, I punched in her number.

I let the phone ring twelve times before I hung up. Now what?

I suddenly realized that I had been at North Beach for over two weeks. I hadn't received a single phone call or a single letter.

Why hadn't any of my friends written to me?

A cold shiver ran down my back. Did my friends all think I was dead? Is that why they hadn't written?

That's impossible, I told myself. Impossible.

At eleven o'clock May-Ann still hadn't returned.

I listened to some tapes on my Walkman and tried to start my mystery novel again.

A little after twelve, I tucked myself into bed and fell into a restless sleep.

I don't know how long I slept. When I woke up, the room was pitch-black.

I stared groggily up at the ceiling as I heard the whispered voice outside my door. *"Lindsay— Lindsay—come out here."*

Chapter 32

LINDSAY

"Who's there?" I called sharply.

I lowered my feet to the floor and made my way unsteadily toward the closed door.

Silence out in the hall.

"Who's there?" I repeated. I held my breath and listened.

"Lindsay—please come." A soft whisper, so soft I could barely hear it over the pounding of my heart.

I slipped on my robe and glanced around the dark room. Where was May-Ann?

"Lindsay—please. Lindsay—"

I pulled the door open and stuck my head out into the hallway.

No one there.

The air in the hall was hot and smelled stale. I

stepped out and silently closed the door behind me. "Who's there?"

No answer.

"May-Ann?" I called.

No answer.

I felt a cold chill at the back of my neck. I pulled the collar of my robe up and tightened the belt.

"Lindsay—please come." A whispered plea from the doorway that led out to the pool.

Should I follow it?

I knew I shouldn't.

But I couldn't help myself.

There were so many mysteries in my life, so many frightening puzzles. Perhaps this was one I could solve.

I followed the whispers to the glass door. I could see the swimming pool under the black sky, the water bright and sparkling under the floodlights.

I pushed the door open and stepped outside. A warm wind swirled around me, catching my light robe, fluttering my unbrushed hair. The trees beyond the pool area shook and whispered.

I stopped halfway to the pool. The trees seemed to be whispering to me: "Stay away—stay away—"

A shudder ran down my body as I stared at the still blue water. I expected to see the girl in the blue bikini. The girl floating facedown in the water.

But the pool was empty.

"Lindsay—please come. Follow me, Lindsay." Another whispered plea, soft as a breeze.

I hesitated.

Was I imagining the voice? Was I really hearing it? Was it coming from inside my mind?

No.

It led me along the back of the guest house. I passed the darkened dining room, then the rooms on the far side.

"Lindsay—hurry."

Where was the voice leading me?

A rectangle of light stretched across the path. My eyes followed the light to the window of the exercise building.

Why were the lights on in there?

I stopped and listened, holding my robe together in the swirling, whispering wind.

"Lindsay—please come." From the door to the weight room.

I turned off the path and made my way toward the voice. The grass felt cold and wet under my bare feet. "Who's there?" I called shrilly. "What do you want?"

I pulled open the door to the weight room and peered inside.

All the overhead lights were on, making the room as bright as day. The air felt hot and sticky. The room smelled of stale sweat.

Black weights were stacked against one wall. The silver weight machines glowed in the bright light.

I took a step across the linoleum floor, my eyes searching the room. "Is anybody in here?" My voice sounded loud and harsh in the small room. "Who's in here?"

Silence.

Then I saw Pug. He was lying on his back between two weight machines.

"Pug—what are you *doing?*" I cried. "It's so late!"

I hurried across the floor to him, my bare feet wet against the linoleum.

"Ohhhh—noooooo." A low wail escaped my lips.

Pug's eyes stared up at me lifelessly. His mouth was open in a frozen, silent cry for help.

"Noooooooo," I moaned.

A barbell stretched over his neck. The bar between the weights pressed down on his throat, choking off his air, crushing him, suffocating him.

Pug was dead.

Panting loudly, I bent down and tried to lift the barbell off him. I knew it was too late. I knew he was dead.

It was an act of panic. I didn't really know what I was doing.

I was still struggling with the barbell when I heard footsteps behind me and realized someone else was in the room.

Uttering a cry of surprise, I let go of the barbell and spun around. "Pete!" I cried. "What are *you* doing here?"

PART FOUR

THE GHOST REVEALED

Chapter 33

LINDSAY

The police arrived quickly, the flashing red lights on their cruisers cutting through the black night.

They grimly went about their work, talking in hushed tones among themselves as they swarmed around the weight room and the grounds outside it. I recognized some of the faces from the night of Cassie's death. Officer Malone, the young woman, was back. She was making notes on her little pad as she talked with Pete.

The other lifeguards had been summoned. They all stood against one wall, looking on in grim silence.

Deirdre was crying again, leaning against a stack of weights, her hands over her face. They had found May-Ann. She was pale and drawn, her eyes narrow slits, her auburn hair flat and damp.

Danny and Arnie hunched in the corner. Danny

looked dazed. Arnie kept tapping his hand nervously against the wall.

Spencer stood close beside me, as if ready to catch me if I fell. I couldn't stop shaking. My entire body felt chilled despite the heat of the room.

"I was walking to my room to go to bed, and I saw the lights on in the weight room," I overheard Pete explaining to Officer Malone. "The lights shouldn't be on so late. I went to investigate. When I went inside, I saw Lindsay. I didn't know what she was doing at first. I saw her lifting a barbell off the floor. Then—" His voice broke. "Then I saw Pug."

Officer Malone turned to me. Her eyes locked on mine. I stared back at her for a moment. Then I turned away.

Is she accusing me? I wondered, shaking even harder. Is that an accusing stare?

Does she think I killed Pug?

Does Pete think I did it?

I stared down at Pug's body. The barbell had been lifted off, but the body hadn't been moved. Pug still stared up blankly, his mouth open in frozen horror.

As I gazed down at him, I saw a black spider crawling slowly across his forehead. "Ohhh." I let out a long sigh. I wanted to brush the spider away.

Pug couldn't do it. I wanted to brush the spider off for him.

Spencer grabbed my arm. "Are you okay?" he whispered, bringing his face close to mine, so close his dark hair brushed against my cheek.

"I—I can't stop shaking," I told him.

My eyes were on the spider climbing down Pug's

forehead. It slid down Pug's cheek—then crawled into his nose.

I let out another moan. My stomach heaved violently. And I bent over and vomited.

Half an hour later. The police had ordered us to the common room. We were sitting on the couch and chairs as Officer Malone questioned us. I was curled up on a leather armchair, my legs tucked beneath me.

Danny had brought me a blue wool blanket, which I wrapped around myself. I felt warmer, but I still couldn't stop shaking.

Spencer returned from the kitchen with a cup of hot tea for me. I tried sipping it, but my hand was shaking too badly to hold the cup steady.

Get a grip, Lindsay, I kept repeating to myself.

No one thinks you're a murderer. Get a grip.

I took a sip of the tea, holding the cup in both hands. The hot steam rose up and felt soothing against my face.

When I glanced up, I found Officer Malone staring at me, chewing her lower lip. "You say you heard the mysterious voice again?" she asked. Her voice revealed no emotion at all. It was as if she were asking if I liked lemon in my tea.

I nodded and pulled the blanket tighter around me.

"You didn't recognize the voice?" Officer Malone asked, expressionless, chewing her lip.

"No," I choked out.

"Why did you follow it?"

My mouth dropped open. I closed it. I stared back at her. "I don't know," I told her.

She lowered her pad. "You don't know why? You heard a whispered voice and you followed it—*again* —knowing that the first time it led you to a murdered girl?"

I shut my eyes. "I just followed it," I said. "It—it pleaded with me. It told me to hurry. I—I—"

I opened my eyes. Angry words burst from my throat. "You don't believe me—do you!" I cried. "You think I'm making up the voice. You think I killed Pug! You think I killed them both!"

"Now, wait—" Officer Malone held up a hand, motioning for me to stop.

"I had no reason to kill Pug!" I screamed. "No reason at all!"

"Well, someone had a reason," a man's voice called from the doorway. A young police officer with red cheeks and curly blond hair falling out from under his cap stepped up beside Officer Malone. "Someone had a reason. Someone seems to be killing you off one by one."

He muttered something to Officer Malone. Then he narrowed his eyes at me.

"Trent, did you get a time of death?" she asked him.

"Martin says the boy has been dead at least an hour," Officer Trent replied, still staring at me.

I shivered and tried to slide under the blanket.

"How come you look familiar to me?" Officer Trent asked, taking a few steps toward me.

I had a sudden impulse to scream: *Because I drowned in the swimming pool here two years ago!*

Instead, I shook my head. "I don't know," I murmured. "I was a lifeguard here before."

"Do you come from around here?" Officer Trent asked, swiping a fly off his broad forehead.

As I started to answer, I heard Officer Malone begin to question May-Ann. "Did Lindsay get along with Pug?" she asked. "Did Lindsay have any arguments with Pug, any strong disagreements?"

I turned from Officer Trent to hear May-Ann's reply.

She shifted uncomfortably in her chair. "No," May-Ann said thoughtfully, twisting and untwisting a strand of auburn hair. "Lindsay told you the truth. Lindsay had no reason, no reason at all to kill Pug."

Officer Malone nodded and started to turn to Danny.

But May-Ann had more to say. "I'll tell you something kind of weird," she continued, still twisting her hair between her fingers.

"What's that?" Officer Malone asked. Officer Trent turned his full attention on May-Ann too.

"Well," May-Ann began slowly, "this evening, a little bit after dinner, Pug and I were talking. We were on the path right outside the weight room." She hesitated.

"And?" Officer Trent demanded impatiently.

"Well, as I was talking to Pug," May-Ann continued, "I looked up—and I saw Lindsay. She was hiding behind a hedge. And she was staring at Pug and me. Just staring at us, with this strange expression on her face."

Chapter 34

MOUSE

*H*ey, Terry. It's me, Mouse.

Score two for me—none for them. Ha-ha.

Another one for you, Terry.

Yeah. His name is Pug. I mean, his name *was* Pug.

Whoa! I'm so excited, Terry. It gets me so excited. It's so hard not to jump up and down and dance and sing.

But I hold it in somehow.

I hold it in and put a real heavy-duty solemn look on my face as soon as the police arrive. No. No one can guess that it's me.

No way, Terry.

Poor Pug. He had a real weight problem!

Ha-ha! That's a joke.

He was a joke.

148

Hey, don't worry about him. Pug was a real pain. Really. Always shooting his mouth off.

Well, he isn't shooting it off anymore.

You would've hated him, Terry. I did.

He was your typical lifeguard. Big and blond. Always showing off, flexing for the girls.

I got him for you, Terry.

And I'm not finished. I've got the next one picked out.

Okay. Well, I'll call you when I finish the next one.

I know you can't call me.

I hear only a dial tone. But I know you're there, Terry.

Later, okay?

Chapter 35

LINDSAY

I had to get away.

The club had been closed for a day while the police did their work. They covered every inch of the grounds, searching for clues, I guess. And they questioned us all endlessly.

After the club opened again, we tried to pretend we could return to normal. But we only went through the motions, like robots.

Meals were quiet and uncomfortable. After dinner, the others disappeared into town, splitting up, going off on their own. I think we were all avoiding one another, avoiding talking about what had happened.

From time to time I'd catch someone staring at me. They'd instantly turn away as soon as I caught them.

I knew what they were thinking.

They were thinking—did she kill Cassie and Pug?

Did she?

Four nights after Pug's murder, Pete tried to give us a pep talk at the dining room table. He told us the summer was just starting and that all the trouble was over.

Did anyone believe him? I don't think so.

Danny asked if Cassie and Pug were being replaced. Pete said he was working on it.

He told us the police had a new theory. They think that someone may have climbed over the fence those two nights, broke onto the grounds, and killed the lifeguards.

I realized I didn't believe that. Sitting there, listening to Pete, I knew all at once that one of us *had* to be the killer.

One of us at the table.

I hadn't thought this till that very moment. I guess it was such a frightening idea that I shut it out of my mind.

I knew that I wasn't the murderer. Even though I was sure the police suspected me.

My eyes went around the table, from face to face. Pete, Danny, Deirdre, Arnie, Spencer, May-Ann . . .

Was one of them really that cold, that crazy, that— dangerous?

I had to get away.

Away from the faces. Away from the club and the lifeguards and—everything.

I borrowed Danny's car. He gave me this intense look as he handed me the keys. "Be careful, okay?" he said softly.

A few minutes later I was heading out onto the highway. Where was I going? I didn't know. Or care.

I just had to drive.

I lowered all the windows and let the hot breeze blow over me. It was a sultry, steamy evening. One of those wet summer nights when everything sticks to everything and your whole body feels soggy and heavy.

I didn't care. The hot air felt great against my face.

I lowered my foot on the gas pedal and got the little Corolla up to near seventy.

The highway was nearly deserted. I passed a big, slow-moving truck and a couple of vans. Flat farmland stretched out on both sides of me, pink under the setting sun.

The hot wind roared through the car.

I reached forward for the knob to turn the radio on—and caught a glimpse of a face in the rearview mirror.

A face leaning toward me from the backseat.

Chapter 36

LINDSAY

The car screeched out of control.

I heard the loud, angry honk of a horn behind me.

My head hit the roof as the car bounced onto the grassy shoulder. My heart standing still, I turned the wheel—and somehow got back on the road.

"Arnie—what— What are you *doing* back there?" I choked out, glaring at him furiously in the rearview mirror.

"Sorry," he said. But his grin didn't fade. "Didn't mean to scare you."

"You—you nearly got us both killed!" I shrieked. "Why did you hide back there?"

He leaned forward. I could feel his hot breath on the back of my neck. It really gave me the creeps.

I had both hands clamped on top of the wheel. I tried to concentrate on calming down and driving safely. But I was so furious, I just wanted to punch him and wipe that silly grin off his weaselly little face.

"I thought I'd come along," Arnie said. "You know. Maybe cheer you up."

"Cheer me up?" I shrieked. "Cheer me up by *killing* us both?"

"Whoa. Calm down, Lindsay," he said. "I'm on *your* side."

"What's that supposed to mean?" I snapped.

"I don't care what the others think," Arnie replied. "I don't think you're a murderer." He let out a high-pitched giggle.

His laugh gave me the chills.

"Is *that* how you plan to cheer me up?" I asked sarcastically.

He frightened me, I realized.

He stood up and climbed over into the passenger seat. "You should give me a chance," he said flatly. "I mean, I like you, Lindsay. And I think you like me."

"Listen, Arnie—" I started to say.

But he grabbed my arm. "I can tell you like me," he said breathlessly.

His grip tightened on my arm.

"That's enough!" I cried.

I hit the brake and guided the car onto the shoulder. We bounced hard, the tires slipping over tall grass.

Before the car came to a stop, I threw open my door.

"Hey!" Arnie called angrily.

But I was already outside. My heart pounding, I crossed in front of the car and jerked open Arnie's door.

"Get out!" I screamed.

"Huh?" His eyes bulged wide with surprise.

A truck roared by with a rush of hot wind.

"Get out!" I repeated. "I mean it, Arnie. If you don't get out, I'm going to flag down a truck. I'm going to get the police."

"But, Lindsay—" He began to object.

I grabbed his arm and tried to pull him out of the car.

He pulled back. His eyes narrowed and his face twisted into an ugly sneer. "You're making a big mistake, Lindsay," he said. "A really big mistake."

Chapter 37

DANNY

I was worried about Lindsay. It was nearly midnight, and she hadn't returned with my car.

Arnie was missing too. Spencer thought maybe he went into town. But no one remembered seeing him leave.

"Hey, Danny—think fast!" May-Ann shouted.

A rubber ball bounced against my head before I could raise my hands from the water. Everyone laughed.

I paddled over to the ball, which was bobbing on top of the water, and heaved it as hard as I could back at May-Ann. Laughing, she caught it easily.

"Over here!" Deirdre shouted. She was wearing a tiny blue bikini that she never wore during the day—and she looked totally awesome!

Just as Deirdre went up to grab the ball, Spencer

grabbed her around the waist and spun her back down into the water. The ball sailed over Deirdre's head. They both came up laughing and sputtering.

I was glad to see everyone unwinding, having a good time for a change. It was such a humid night—like living in a steam bath.

Spencer and I had been playing poker for hours. We knew we could never get to sleep. We jumped into the pool, trying to cool off. A few minutes later Deirdre, Pete, and May-Ann had joined us.

We were splashing around, having silly floating competitions, tossing the ball around. Just generally goofing. It was great.

But then a little before midnight I realized that Lindsay wasn't back. And I had a gnawing feeling at the pit of my stomach, a slightly uncomfortable, nervous feeling.

I was up on the diving board, ready to show off my fabulous reverse cannonball, when Lindsay finally came through the gate. I called to her.

She waved and started toward the guest house.

"Hey—come over here!" I shouted. I jumped down from the diving board.

She hesitated.

"Come on—jump in!" Spencer shouted to Lindsay.

She laughed. "I'm dressed!"

"So what?" he shouted back.

I trotted over to her. "Everything okay?" I asked.

She nodded. "Sort of." She twirled my car keys in her hand. "I had a little problem with Arnie," she said, making a face.

"Arnie? Where is he?" I asked, confused. I was

dripping water on her sneakers, I saw. So I took a step back.

"He's enjoying a nice walk back," Lindsay replied dryly.

"I don't get it," I confessed.

"He hid in the backseat. He nearly scared me to death. I dropped him off," she said, sighing. "On the highway. He'll probably hitch a ride. He'll be here soon. I hadn't driven that far."

I shook my head. "Weird," I muttered.

"Lindsay—get changed!" Spencer called. "Come on in and cool off!"

"The water's great!" Pete called to her. He started to shout something else, but May-Ann ducked his head under the water, starting a playful wrestling match.

Deirdre performed a perfect swan dive. Everyone applauded.

"Maybe I will get changed," Lindsay said, talking more to herself than to me. "I'm totally drenched." She shook her head. Her hair was all windblown, and her forehead was all sweaty. But she looked really excellent to me.

"What a night," she mumbled. "Back in a minute." She headed off to get changed.

I watched her disappear inside. I was thinking about Arnie, stranded on the highway. Bet he won't be in a good mood when he gets back, I thought.

Back in the pool, Spencer and Pete were working on their butterfly strokes. Pete was smaller than Spencer, but he was a stronger swimmer.

I jumped in, eager to join them. My butterfly is pitiful. I need all the help I can get!

Deirdre and May-Ann had climbed out and were heading to the diving board, laughing together about something.

Lindsay appeared a few seconds later in a one-piece black swimsuit. Without hesitating, she stepped up to the side of the pool at the deep end, and plunged in.

I flashed her a smile as she surfaced. "Feel better?"

"This is the life!" she called back.

"It doesn't get any better than this!" Spencer chimed in.

Lindsay started swimming slow, steady laps. She had a good stroke, I saw, but she held her head too high out of the water.

"Come on, Danny—butterfly race. Two laps!" Pete called.

I nodded and swam over to line up.

Up at the edge of the pool, I glimpsed Deirdre and May-Ann laughing and goofing around.

Deirdre reached up to adjust the straps around her neck—and May-Ann swiped at them, trying to pull the bikini top off.

"Hey—watch it!" Deirdre cried, laughing.

They wrestled some more. Then Deirdre let out a squeal of surprise as May-Ann pushed her into the pool.

Deirdre sank with a huge splash.

Spencer, Pete, and I laughed and applauded.

Standing on the pool edge, May-Ann took a low bow.

Then, as Deirdre surfaced, sputtering and choking, I heard a shrill scream.

I spun around, startled.

It took me a little while to realize it was Lindsay.

She was screaming her head off. The strangest, most frightening scream I'd ever heard.

Relentless high-pitched howls. Like an animal caught in a trap.

Spencer got to her first. I came up on her other side.

We both dragged her, screaming still, to the side of the pool in the shallow end.

"Lindsay! Lindsay—what's wrong? What *is* it?" I cried.

She kept shrieking. She didn't seem to hear me.

"Lindsay! Lindsay!" Spencer shouted, grabbing her shoulders.

Her entire body shuddered. *"I'm not Lindsay!"* she sobbed.

The others all huddled around. "What's wrong with her? What is she saying?" May-Ann asked, hands at her waist, staring down at us from the pool edge.

"I'm not Lindsay!" Lindsay screamed again.

"Lindsay—take a deep breath," Pete instructed her. "Lindsay—listen to me. Take a deep breath and—"

"I'm not Lindsay!" she cried shrilly. "My memory —it came back to me when—when May-Ann pushed Deirdre in. It all came back to me."

She was breathing hard, her chest heaving up and down, sort of sobbing with each breath.

"Lindsay—" Pete said, his voice low and calm. "Lindsay—listen to me—"

"But I'm *not* Lindsay!" she insisted. "Lindsay is dead!"

May-Ann gasped.

I felt a chill run down my back.

"I'm Marissa!" Lindsay cried. "Marissa Dunton. I *killed* Lindsay two years ago!"

Chapter 38

MARISSA

Danny and Spencer walked me to the common room in the guest house. They were both being so nice to me. Danny wrapped a big beach towel around my shoulders. Spencer hurried to my room and brought me back a white terry-cloth robe.

I felt so strange. Excited and relieved, confused and frightened—all at the same time.

At least now I knew who I was. Now I knew I wasn't Lindsay Beck. I wasn't the dead lifeguard.

It had all come back to me in a single flash of vivid memory.

It had happened two summers ago. A summer of horror—horror that still hadn't ended.

Two summers ago. But now the memory was so strong, so bright, so real to me, I felt it had all happened yesterday.

Spencer and Danny huddled close to me on the leather couch. "Do you want to talk about it?" Danny asked.

"I guess," I replied uncertainly. I felt so mixed up, so totally wired, I decided it might make me feel better to tell them the story, to get it out.

"You were a lifeguard here last summer?" Danny asked. His eyes locked on mine.

"No, not last summer," I told him. "Two summers ago. Lindsay Beck was a lifeguard that summer too. Lindsay and I were friends. We were roommates in the lifeguard dorm. She was from Shadyside too."

I pulled the robe tighter and stuffed my hands into the big pockets. "We weren't best best friends," I continued, picturing Lindsay, poor Lindsay, as I talked. "But we were friends. One afternoon, soon after the club opened, Lindsay and I had a stupid argument."

"What about?" Spencer broke in, running a hand back through his dark wet hair.

I shrugged. "I don't even remember. Something really dumb and unimportant," I replied. "We were standing at the edge of the pool—near where May-Ann and Deirdre were standing tonight. We started wrestling, playfully at first. But it quickly got more intense."

I sighed. The memory was so strong, so overwhelmingly horrible. "Lindsay was wearing a blue bikini. I shoved her. I didn't mean to hurt her or anything. I was angry, but I never meant to hurt her. . . ." My voice trailed off as I relived the terrible moment.

"She fell into the pool?" Danny asked softly.

I nodded. "She fell. She hit her head on the side. On the concrete. Her head—it split open. She sank into the pool. The water—the blue water filled with blood. It was an accident. A horrible accident."

I wiped the tears from my eyes with the sleeve of the robe. I was breathing hard, my heart pounding.

"She died?" Danny asked hesitantly after a long silence.

I nodded. "She died."

I stared straight ahead. The room, the furniture, the diving posters on the wall—all became a soft blur.

"I was in a hospital for a long time after that," I told them.

"Marissa—if this is too painful . . ." Danny started to say.

I shook my head. "I want to get it out," I told him. "I want to get the whole story out. I think I'll feel better if I do."

Spencer brought me a cup of cold water from the water cooler in the corner. I gulped it down. Then I continued.

"I had to go to a mental hospital. Because after the accident—after the accident I assumed Lindsay's identity."

I saw the surprise on the boys' faces. I turned my eyes straight ahead to the wall. My voice came out low and steady.

"I thought I was Lindsay. I really believed I was Lindsay. I guess I felt so guilty—so guilty that I had to bring her back to life. So I *became* her. I brought Lindsay back to life by becoming her. I had taken a lot of her stuff after her death from our dorm room. I wore her clothes and used her things—I really thought they were mine. That I was *her*.

"I was in the hospital for several months," I continued. "I don't really remember how long. Eventually, I got better. I became myself—Marissa—again. The doctors worked hard to remove my guilt. They tried to make me realize that Lindsay's death was an accident—a tragic accident. That I couldn't blame myself for the rest of my life."

I turned from Danny to Spencer. Danny had his head lowered, a solemn expression on his usually cheerful face. Spencer tapped his hand on the arm of the couch. He avoided my glance.

"So they sent me home to my parents," I continued with a sigh. "I had missed an entire school year, and last summer—it was gone too. All that time was gone. But I was glad to be home in Shadyside. And things went okay for this past school year. But—"

I swallowed hard. I was so eager to tell the story, I thought it would be easy. But it was so difficult, so painful to be living it again as I told it.

I took a deep breath. "I guess the hospital sent me home too soon. I guess I wasn't ready, wasn't ready to be Marissa full-time. I ran away from home this summer. I just sneaked out early one morning."

"You mean your parents don't know you're here?" Spencer asked.

I shook my head. I pictured my parents. They must be so worried, so frantic. My poor parents. They've had so much sadness, all because of me.

"I sneaked out," I repeated, removing my hands from the robe pocket and wrapping them around my chest in a tight, protective hug. "I became Lindsay again, and I sneaked out. I got a bus from Shadyside. And I came back here. I came back here thinking I was Lindsay. Thinking I was supposed to be a lifeguard again."

I sighed. "Why did I come back? I don't know. I don't really know. I guess I had to come back to the place where I had killed Lindsay."

The story was finished. I settled back on the couch, my arms still wrapped around myself, hot tears rolling down my cheeks.

A heavy silence fell over the room. No one spoke. No one moved.

Finally Spencer broke the silence. He turned to me, his dark eyes probing mine. "I—I just don't understand one thing," he said hesitantly. "Why did you kill Cassie and Pug?"

The question sent a cold shiver down my back.

"I don't know," I told him.

Chapter 39

MARISSA

I stared at Spencer blankly. His question had caught me completely by surprise.

Danny had a startled expression on his face too.

I jumped to my feet and stared down at Spencer. "I *didn't* kill them!" I cried shrilly. Then I added, "At least, I don't remember."

"You didn't remember who you were," Spencer said thoughtfully. "Maybe you killed them and blocked that memory away too."

"No!" I protested, pressing my hands against my waist. "Why are you *saying* that? Why would I kill them? I had no reason—"

I stopped.

I suddenly remembered something.

Standing in front of Spencer. "Whoa—hold on a minute, Spencer," I said, thinking hard. "You said

167

you were here at the club that summer. You said you recognized me."

"Yes, but—" Spencer began. His dark eyes flashed. His cheeks turned red.

"Why didn't you call me Marissa?" I demanded. "Why didn't you say something when I told you my name was Lindsay?"

He raised both hands as if holding me back. "I didn't really remember," he said. "I'm sorry. I'm really sorry."

"But, Spencer—" I interrupted.

"It was such a crazy summer, Marissa," Spencer continued. "I had just arrived. The club had been open for only a few days, and everyone was just getting settled. Suddenly one girl lifeguard was dead and another one was taken away. I remembered seeing you. But then you were gone, and I didn't really remember your name. I didn't remember which one you were. I'm sorry."

I studied his expression. He seemed really embarrassed.

Suddenly Danny got to his feet. "I have to go tell Pete about this," he said. He glanced out the window to the pool area. It was quiet outside. "Guess everyone has gone to bed. Well, I'd better wake Pete. I think he'd want to know about this."

"I've got to call my parents!" I cried. "I've got to call them right away and tell them I'm okay!"

"Use the phone in Pete's office," Danny said, pointing in the right direction. "It'll be totally private. They'll sure be glad to hear from you." He smiled at me and tossed his towel over his shoulder. "Glad you're getting things straight, Lindsay—I mean Marissa."

Spencer gazed up at me from the couch. "Do you want me to come with you?" he asked with concern. "Will you be okay?"

"I'll be okay," I told him. "I'll call home. Then I'll go to bed. Thanks, Spencer."

He and Danny disappeared out the door. I made my way to Pete's office.

I was so excited, I couldn't think clearly. Everything passed by in a blur.

What should I say to Mom and Dad? I wondered. How can I explain what happened?

I knew my mother would burst into happy tears and not be able to say a word. But what would my dad say?

They must think I'm dead somewhere, I realized with a shudder. I've been away almost two weeks. I didn't leave them a note. I didn't leave a hint about where I was going.

I felt so bad for them.

How could I cause them so much pain?

My heart pounding, I darted into Pete's office and clicked on the ceiling light. Then I made my way to his desk and reached for the phone.

Before I could pick up the receiver, I heard footsteps. I glanced over to see Spencer stop in the doorway.

"Marissa, are you okay?" he asked. "Telling that story must have been so upsetting to you. I just wanted to make sure you were all right."

"Thanks," I said, forcing a smile. "I'm okay. Really. I'm just trying to figure out how to tell my parents—"

169

Before I could finish my sentence, the phone rang. I cried out, startled.

Spencer took a few steps into the room. "Who could be calling after midnight?"

I picked up the receiver and heard a woman's voice. I could tell instantly that she was very stressed out. "Is this the North Beach Country Club?" she asked.

Pete's speakerphone was on. Spencer and I could both hear her.

"Yes, it is," I replied.

"This is Mrs. Brown," the woman said. "I must apologize for not calling sooner. You all must be wondering why my son Spencer never showed up for his lifeguard job."

Chapter 40

MARISSA

"**H**uh?" I gasped in surprise.

The woman's trembling voice sounded tinny on the speakerphone. "It—it's been so awful," she stammered.

"I don't understand," I told her. "You said that Spencer—"

"He was *murdered!*" Mrs. Brown exclaimed with a sob. "The day before he was supposed to report to the club. I—I know I should have called sooner. But I haven't been able to do anything."

There was a long pause. I could hear her shallow breathing. She was trying to keep herself together.

Finally she continued. "I was in shock. The doctors —they had to sedate me. I've lost all track of time. I don't know if it's day or night."

"That's okay," I said shakily. "I understand. I—"

"I'm so sorry," she broke in, starting to cry. "Spencer—my boy—he's dead. I thought I should call you. He was a good boy. He would have made a good lifeguard. He—"

She burst into loud sobs. The line went dead.

I stared down at the phone, feeling totally confused. Then I turned my eyes to the doorway. "Spencer—what did she mean?" I asked.

But he was gone.

I dashed out into the hall. "Spencer?"

I could hear footsteps. Running. Down the hall, I saw a shadow dart around the corner.

"Spencer?"

I started to run after it. The woman's heartbreaking sobs echoed in my ears.

What did she mean? Why did she say Spencer was dead?

I turned the corner, breathing hard. No one there.

The glass door led to the pool area. Had he gone out this way?

I pushed the door open and stepped outside. The night was hot and still. The pool was empty, the water sparkling under the white floodlights. The other lifeguards had all gone to bed.

"Spencer?" I tried to call to him, but my voice came out a hushed whisper. "Spencer?" The sound seemed to bounce off the pavement and hover in the heavy, wet night air.

I took a few uncertain steps toward the pool, searching for him, squinting into the bright light.

His shadow fell over me as he leapt out in front of me, blocking my path. His dark eyes burned into

172

mine. His expression was hard, his jaw clenching and unclenching.

"Spencer—what did that woman mean?" I blurted out. "Why did she say Spencer was dead?"

"Spencer *had* to die," he said softly, so soft the words barely reached me. "I had to be a lifeguard. For Terry. Spencer died so I could be the lifeguard."

He took a step closer to me. The darkness of his shadow fell over me. "And now, Marissa, you have to die too," he said.

Chapter 41

MARISSA

I still didn't understand. I guess I didn't want to believe what he was saying.

"You—you're going to *kill* me?" I shrieked, more in disbelief than in fear.

His dark eyes remained on mine, unblinking. When he spoke, he sounded so calm. "I have to kill you, Marissa. You know too much. Anyway, it's your turn. I already made the choice. You were always going to be next."

"You—you killed Cassie and Pug?" I stammered. I took a step back, stumbling over a deck chair.

A wave of fear swept over me. I finally realized the danger I was in.

He nodded. "See? You know too much," he said, still calm. "And sooner or later your memory will come back totally—then you'll *really* remember who I am."

As he said those words, I *did* remember him.

It was as if a curtain lifted. The dark shadow faded from my eyes.

"You're not Spencer—you're Jack," I murmured.

Yes. I remembered him.

Jack Mouser. Everyone called him Mouse.

"You—you were here two years ago," I stammered, pointing at him, remembering, remembering everything so clearly now. "You were here, Jack—but you weren't a lifeguard."

A strange, bitter smile formed on his face. "That's right, Marissa," he said softly. "Terry and I, we worked in the kitchen. We *wanted* to be lifeguards. Man, did we *want* to be lifeguards."

The bitter smile became a sneer. "But we were Terry and Mouse, the kitchen dudes."

"And we teased you." I remembered. "We made fun of you, didn't we? You were so eager to be lifeguards. We made you think—"

"You made us think we could be lifeguards," he said, his voice suddenly rising in anger. "Your lifeguard friends told Terry and me you could certify us. Remember? Remember all the things you made us do?"

I did remember. We were pretty hard on the two of them. We thought it was such a riot.

"You made us do twenty dives each one night, remember?" Mouse demanded angrily. "You made

175

Terry and me drop to the bottom of the pool and hold our breath till we almost drowned. You made us run fifty laps around the pool in flipflops."

Yes. I remembered.

"It was all a joke," he murmured, glaring at me with such hatred I had to lower my eyes. "All a cruel joke. After Terry and I did everything, after we passed your *test*—then you told us we were total jerks. You were only kidding. You couldn't certify us. You—" His voice caught in his throat.

"It was mean," I admitted, still avoiding his stare. "It was really mean, Mouse. But it was just a joke."

"Just a joke?" he screamed, losing control. "Just a joke? Listen to me, Marissa. Terry was a messed-up dude. Terry was a great guy. He was my best friend. But he was a messed-up dude."

"What do you mean?" I asked hesitantly.

"He had problems," Mouse replied bitterly. "Terry had a lot of personal problems. Last summer he tried out for lifeguard, and he was rejected. He was messed up, Marissa. He couldn't take being rejected. He had too many other problems. He went home, and he killed himself."

"Oh!" A loud, startled cry escaped from my throat. "I'm so sorry, Mouse. But you can't blame—"

"So I came to pay the lifeguards back," Mouse said, lowering his voice again. "One by one."

"But we're not the same lifeguards!" I protested.

"I'm not crazy!" he shot back. "I know that. But I don't care. Terry doesn't care either. They're lifeguards, Marissa—and they're all going to die."

"But, Mouse!" I protested, taking a step back.

"Bye, Marissa," he said quietly, quietly and calmly. "Bye, Marissa. It's your turn now."

Chapter 42

MARISSA

"Mouse, wait—" I cried, raising both hands as if to shield myself.

He shook his head. The coldest smile spread over his face, the coldest, cruelest smile I had ever seen.

"Mouse, please?" I searched the entire pool area.

Where was Danny? Where was Pete?

Where was anyone who could help me?

It grew so silent, so eerily silent. All I could hear was the soft splash of the water against the sides of the pool—and the violent beating of my heart.

"Mouse—let me go!" I cried, my voice just above a hushed whisper.

"I was so happy to see you here when I arrived," Mouse continued, ignoring me. "I was so happy to see that you were messed up too, that you didn't even know your own name. It was such a lucky break for me. I could kill the lifeguards and make everyone think you did it."

"You mean—" I hesitated. *"You* were the one whispering to me? *You* were the one calling me to Cassie and Pug?"

He nodded. "Enough talk. Bye, Marissa."

I tried to get away, but I ran into another deck chair.

He grabbed me around the waist. His other hand pulled my hair. He twisted me. Yanked my head back. Dragged me.

I tried to struggle away. But he was stronger than he looked.

Too strong.

I tried to call for help. But he slid a hand over my mouth.

I twisted and tried to kick at him. I tried to bite his hand.

But he was too strong, too strong.

He dragged me toward the pool.

The pavement slipped out from under me. I plunged down. The water rose up over my head. So cold.

Leaning over the pool edge, he held me down. One hand held my shoulder. The other hand gripped my hair. He pushed my head down.

I thrashed my arms frantically. I couldn't get free.

He held me under. I couldn't breathe.

I kicked and swung my arms. But he held on tight. Held me under.

Held me under until my lungs were about to burst.

The water felt so cold. So freezing cold.

I struggled to get away from him. But I was losing strength.

My chest—my chest—

I'm going to drown, I told myself.

Chapter 43

MARISSA

Drowning . . . drowning . . .

My body went limp.

I stopped struggling.

My arms slid weakly down to my sides.

Slowly Mouse let go of my shoulder. Then I felt his hand loosen its grip on my head.

As soon as I knew I was floating free, I raised my arms and pulled myself to the surface.

I saw Mouse, his back to the pool now. He turned suddenly, gaping at me in surprise.

At that instant I could see in his face that he knew I had faked it. I'd pretended to drown so he'd let go.

Now, before he could get away, I thrust myself up and reached out. I grabbed his ankles and pulled.

Pulled him on top of me into the water.

He tried to punch me with his fist, but I slid away.

I grabbed his shoulders and shoved him under.

We were groaning and crying out as we wrestled.

He pulled my hair, wrapped his arm around my throat, tried to choke me.

Then suddenly, I heard a cry. A splash.

Mouse turned away from me, startled.

I saw two hands dive at him, grab his face.

I was no longer fighting him alone.

"May-Ann!" I managed to gasp.

She grasped Mouse in a tight choke hold. I pinned his arms behind him.

Together we dragged him to the shallow end.

I saw Danny and Deirdre running across the pavement to help us. Arnie was behind them. He was still in his street clothes. He must have just gotten back.

We all held Mouse down. Danny sent Arnie to call the police.

"Did Spencer kill Cassie and Pug?" May-Ann demanded, shaking water from her hair. Her shorts and T-shirt were soaked to her skin. I saw that she had dived in to help me with her sneakers on.

"He isn't Spencer," I told her. "Before summer started, he killed Spencer and took his place. His name is Jack. Jack Mouser. He is the one. He killed them both. He told me."

In the confusion, I hadn't realized that Pete was with us too. He and Danny held Mouse down.

Mouse had given up. He no longer struggled. "I did it for you, Terry," he said loudly, staring up at the sky as if in a daze. "I did it for you. I know you can hear me, Terry."

I stood up. I couldn't stop shivering.

182

May-Ann walked over and wrapped me in a tight hug. "I'm so sorry," she whispered. "I'm so sorry that I suspected you."

I let out a relieved sigh. "I suspected you too," I confessed.

May-Ann let go and took a step back, her expression surprised. "You suspected me?"

"Where *were* you those nights?" I asked. "The nights of the murders."

She brought her face close to mine. "I was with Pete," she whispered. "We've been seeing each other back home. But there's a rule against him dating the lifeguards. He could lose his job. So I sneaked out."

"Is that what you and Pug were arguing about in front of the weight room?" I asked her.

May-Ann nodded. "Pug found out about Pete and me. He was threatening to tell. Just for fun."

I could hear sirens in the parking lot. The police were arriving.

"You girls go get dried off," Danny called.

May-Ann and I walked off toward the guest house arm in arm. "I have to call my parents," I said. "I have to call them right away."

"What are you going to tell them?" she asked, holding open the door.

"That I'm okay," I replied.

About the Author

"Where do you get your ideas?"

That's the question that R. L. Stine is asked most often. "I don't know where my ideas come from," he says. "But I do know that I have a lot more scary stories in my mind that I can't wait to write."

So far, he has written nearly three dozen mysteries and thrillers for young people, all of them bestsellers.

Bob grew up in Columbus, Ohio. Today he lives in an apartment near Central Park in New York City with his wife, Jane, and fourteen-year-old son, Matt.

ONE EVIL SUMMER
(Coming in July 1994)

Amanda Conklin can't wait for summer at the beach, away from the horrors of Fear Street. Sure, summer school is going to be a drag, but at least she doesn't have to take care of her younger brother and sister. Her parents have hired a local teenager—Chrissy Minor—as a mother's helper.

Chrissy seems like the perfect baby-sitter to everyone . . . except Amanda. Amanda doesn't trust Chrissy. Something's wrong with her. Something evil, something dangerous. And Amanda's sure that the beautiful baby-sitter is out to murder her family!

FEAR STREET®

R.L. Stine